Times Squared

Also by Julia DeVillers and Jennifer Roy

TRADING FACES

TAKE TWO

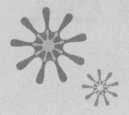

Times Squared

Julia DeVillers
& Jennifer Roy

ALADDIN M!X

NEW YORK   LONDON   TORONTO   SYDNEY   NEW DELHI

ALADDIN M!X

Simon & Schuster Children's Publishing Division

1230 Avenue of the Americas, New York, NY 10020

First Aladdin M!X edition December 2011

Copyright © 2011 by Julia DeVillers and Jennifer Roy

All rights reserved, including the right of reproduction in whole or in part in any form.

ALADDIN is a trademark of Simon & Schuster, Inc.,

and related logo is a registered trademark of Simon & Schuster, Inc.

ALADDIN M!X and related logo are registered trademarks of Simon & Schuster, Inc.

Also available in an Aladdin hardcover edition.

For information about special discounts for bulk purchases, please contact Simon & Schuster Special Sales at 1-866-506-1949 or business@simonandschuster.com.

The Simon & Schuster Speakers Bureau can bring authors to your live event.

For more information or to book an event contact the Simon & Schuster Speakers Bureau at 1-866-248-3049 or visit our website at www.simonspeakers.com.

Designed by Karin Paprocki

The text of this book was set in Granjon.

Manufactured in the United States of America 1111 OFF

2 4 6 8 10 9 7 5 3 1

The Library of Congress has cataloged the hardcover edition as follows:

DeVillers, Julia.

Times squared / Julia DeVillers, Jennifer Roy. — 1st Aladdin hardcover ed.

p. cm.

Summary: Identical twins Payton and Emma have vowed never to switch places again, but they face an emergency while the mathletes and Drama Geckos are all in New York City together.

ISBN 978-1-4169-7532-8 (hc)

[1. Twins—Fiction. 2. Sisters—Fiction. 3. Individuality—Fiction. 4. School field trips—Fiction. 5. Middle schools—Fiction. 6. Schools—Fiction. 7. New York (N.Y.)—Fiction.]

I. Roy, Jennifer Rozines, 1967– II. Title.

PZ7.D4974Tim 2011

[Fic]—dc22

2010026839

ISBN 978-1-4169-6732-3 (pbk)

ISBN 978-1-4424-1728-1 (eBook)

To Quinn Rachel DeVillers,
number one daughter and niece

Payton

One

MIDDLE SCHOOL AFTER LAST PERIOD

Cell phone! My cell phone was ringing. I tossed my books into my locker and scrounged around in my tote bag to answer it. I felt my cocoa-mocha lip gloss. I felt my little tin of mints. Finally I found it—right at the bottom of my bag.

"Hello?" I said into my phone. "Hello?"

Nobody was there. I looked at my phone and didn't see the on light. Wait a minute, I hadn't even turned my phone back on after last period.

But then my ringtone went off again. It was the awesome new ringtone I'd downloaded last night. I looked at my cell phone again, confused.

❀ 1 ❀

"Hello?" a voice said next to me.

It was my twin sister, Emma. She was standing at her locker, talking into her own cell phone.

"Hello, Mom," she was saying. "You can pick Payton and me up today after mathletes and Drama Club? Excellent times two."

It was her cell phone that was ringing? I crossed my arms and waited until she said good-bye and hung up.

"Emma, are you going to explain this?" I said.

"Oh, that was Mom," Emma said. "She can pick us up after mathletes and Drama Club."

"No, I meant explain why you're copying my ringtone," I said. "I thought it was *my* phone that was going off."

It was bad enough to have a twin with an identical face. Couldn't I at least have my own ringtone?

Emma and I are seriously identical. Even our own parents can't tell us apart sometimes. It's hard to have my own identity.

"My ringtone makes a unique statement about me," I said. "Who I am. My individuality. That ringtone is totally *me*."

"Well, your individuality was the number one download on iTunes," Emma said, packing up her humongous backpack. "Some unique statement."

I sighed and pulled out the books I needed to bring home from school.

"Hi, Payton," a girl from my art class said as she walked by with girl I didn't know.

"See, you're a unique individual," Emma said. "That person knew who you were."

Okay, that *was* a good sign.

"Which one is Payton?" I heard the girl I didn't know say as they walked away.

"I don't know," the girl answered. "But one of them has to be, right?"

Sigh. Pretty soon I was just going to wear a name tag. Or a sign over my head that said:

I'm PAYTON, the twin who
- is one inch taller.
- has slightly greener eyes.
- is dressed quite fashionably in her pink sweater, skinny jeans, and tall boots and is about to head to Drama Club.

Drama Club! Yay! It hadn't been yay at first. After Emma and I had switched places our first week of school and gotten busted, we were assigned community service.

I had to clean the storage room underneath the school's stage. It wasn't fun. But community service was over and now I got to be a real part of Drama Club. I had helped out in the play, *The Wizard of Oz*, this weekend. I had gone to the cast party. I even had new friends in Drama Club. Yes, *friends*. Tess, Nick . . .

The friends I always dreamed I'd make in middle school! The first weeks of middle school humiliation had been over and forgotten. Emma and I had been known as the identical twins who switched places, fooled everyone until they were busted, and had been filmed on school television making complete idiots of themselves. We had planned to never trade places again. No more mix-up switch-up! No more flip-flop twin-swap! We were done with that.

Okay, but then we *had* to because Emma had to cover for me onstage. But nobody really knows about that part except us. And Tess and Nick. Oh, and the two identical boys Emma tutored for her community service.

But all of that is in the past!

"Look, it's those twins who got in a fight on live TV," someone said as she passed by with a group of people who started giggling.

Or maybe not totally in the past.

"No, we're not!" Emma yelled down the hall. They turned around and giggled at her.

"Oh my gosh! Shush, Emma!" I said. "And besides, we *are* those twins."

"Actually, that's not accurate," Emma told me. "Technically, it was a school video podcast through a computer setup. Not TV."

Augh. It was hopeless to argue with her. I pulled out my relaxing lavender-scented room-mister and spritzed the inside of my locker. Then I stuck my head inside and took deep breaths so I wouldn't cause another twin scene.

I heard Emma's ringtone go off again. And again. And again.

"Yeesh. Aren't you going to answer that already?" I pulled my head out and asked Emma.

"That's *your* phone," Emma said calmly.

"Agh!" I reached into my tote bag on the floor and checked my cell. Yup, I had missed a call from our mother. "Emma, can you please just change your ringtone? My life is confusing enough."

"I think this ringtone is very *me*," Emma said. Then she paused. "All right, it isn't me at all. But it definitely demonstrates my awareness of the latest music trends."

"Since when do you know or care about music trends?" I asked Emma. Ever since we switched, Emma *had* been starting to get interested in fashion trends for the first time in her life. But music?

"Since I got an A minus in choir." Emma sounded upset. "Choir! It better not ruin my perfect average."

Emma had been trying to get switched out of choir since the first day of school. Honestly, I'd been surprised they hadn't yet kicked her out of it. Emma can do tons of things, but singing is so not one of them.

"My choir teacher is inexplicably into pop music," Emma complained. "Does she care that I know the history of classical *and* medieval music? Apparently not."

"Sorry," I said.

"I told Counselor Case I'd take anything else—advanced math, I'd even tutor the terror twins more days after school," Emma continued.

Wow. She was really serious. The terror twins were Mason and Jason. Their parents were the school's guidance counselor and her husband, the mathletes' coach. The boys were definitely double trouble, but also kind of sweet.

"Counselor Case said no," Emma grumbled. "She said it was good for me to step out of my comfort zone."

"What about the comfort zone of the other people in choir?" I asked. "It's got to be painful for them to hear you sing."

"You are not helpful," Emma replied. "Anyway, I plan to impress her with my knowledge of the trends. I've studied the iTunes and radio charts from the past eighteen months. I've also charted my predictions for what songs will be next and new. I can share with her the statistical probability of . . . blah blah blah."

I tuned her out. I was glad I was put in art class instead of choir. I could make fun of Emma's singing voice all I wanted, but I couldn't sing either. It was something else that was identical about us.

I never, ever sang in public. Like this past weekend the wrap party was held after the play. There was a karaoke machine and people were up there singing. But nope, not me. I've had enough embarrassment lately.

"We could switch places for choir," Emma mused. "It would save me from having to learn those silly pop-music lyrics."

No! I'm never switching places in school again. Never, ever, ever! Switching places definitely had caused way too much trouble.

I heard footsteps behind me. And another noise, like a footstep *clop*, footstep *clop*. I turned around to see what that was. And regretted it.

The reason we had switched in the first place was coming down the hall. Its name was Sydney.

During the first week of middle school, I had thought Sydney would be the "right kind of friend" for me—she was popular and had great clothes and style. Instead it turned out to be the opposite: Sydney was a fake, a mean girl. Especially mean to me.

So when I'd tripped at lunch and my burrito went flying and oozing all over Ox (who I didn't know yet), I was completely humiliated.

That's when the very first twin switch took place. Emma became "me" and dealt with Sydney, while I recovered from the embarrassment.

Since the lunchroom incident of embarrassment, a *lot* had happened. Including Sydney wiping out in her Glinda the Good Witch giant plastic bubble minutes before the Drama Club was about to put on *The Wizard of Oz*. Which led to Sydney on crutches and another twin switch and then finally me performing awesomely as Glinda. My first time acting onstange.

That part was actually pretty cool. The not-so-cool

bit was that Sydney didn't like me before, and she *definitely* didn't like me after I took over her part.

She was walking with someone who did like me, at least. Tess.

"Hi, Payton! Hi, Emma!" Tess said. "Payton, are you ready for Drama Club?"

"One second," I said, tossing a notebook into my backpack.

"Wheeeew," Sydney said, leaning dramatically against the locker next to me. "I'm *exhausted* having to crutch all the way down here to the boonies. But Tess said we had to stop by and pick you up, Payton. Even though the auditorium is the other way."

Sydney wrinkled her nose at me.

"That *is* really nice of Tess," I said. "And also really nice of Tess to carry all of your stuff."

Tess was the one who looked exhausted. She was carrying Sydney's backpack along with her own and a large cardboard box. Tess was always nice. Too nice. She didn't realize that Sydney was trying to lure her into becoming one of the Popular People groupies. Tess was pretty, smart, and had the lead role in our play.

I had been the first recruit because Sydney had liked my designer clothes.

(That didn't work!)

"Okay, let's get going, Payton." Sydney looked right at Emma.

"Oh, that's Emma," Tess said, trying to be helpful.

Sydney knew that.

"Silly me." Sydney fake laughed. "I just can't tell you two twins apart because you're *exactly* alike."

"Identical twins can't be exactly alike," Emma pointed out. "Although our genetic makeup may be the same, environmental factors also play a role."

Emma started going off on some EmmaEncyclopedia babble.

"What are you talking about?" Sydney and I both said at the same time. We shared a moment of solidarity as we both looked at Emma, totally confused.

"It means we're different," Emma said, throwing up her hands. "And, Sydney? It's possible to tell us apart if you *try*."

She looked at Sydney pointedly.

"It's easy to tell them apart today," Tess broke in cheerfully. "Just look at Emma's T-shirt!"

Erg. Tess had to go and point that out. The T-shirt said MATHLETES REGIONAL COMPETITION WINNER! on the front. And it had a cartoon of goofy dancing octagons or pentagons or something-gons.

"Stylish," Sydney said with a smirk.

"Um." I needed to change the subject. I held out my hands. "Tess, I can help you carry Sydney's stuff."

"Thanks." Tess smiled and handed me the cardboard box. "My photography teacher asked me to bring these to Mrs. Burkle. He said not to bend them, though, and—"

But as she was telling me that, Sydney put her crutch down right on my foot. And I yelped! And the box fell open and a bunch of pictures came flying out!

"Oh no!" I cried. And then . . . Oh no.

They were pictures of people's faces from Drama Club.

"Oh, they're our headshots!" Sydney squealed.

We had gotten headshots taken. That was one of our twin-switch times. Sydney had dumped a bucket of dirty water on my head so Emma had pretended to be me for the photos.

And I was staring at the result. There was a picture that said PAYTON MILLS. And on it was Emma's face. Emma had her head crooked at a weird angle.

"Hey, it's me!" Emma said, leaning over.

I elbowed her. Nobody knew about that particular switch.

"I mean, it's *you*!" Emma said quickly to correct herself. "Payton."

"Even they can't tell each other apart." Sydney snorted.

"I must say, Payton, you look better than ever in that picture," Emma said, grinning.

I tried to grab the picture off the floor but Sydney put her crutch on it and stopped me.

"Why is your head crooked?" Sydney laughed.

"It's at a twenty three-degree angle so that the light would reflect off her shiny hair," Emma said. "Duh."

"Then why is her barrette crooked?" Sydney asked. "And oopsie! Your lip gloss is smeared like a mustache. Heh."

I glared at Emma. I used my twin telepathy to yell at her for not checking in the mirror before she got *my* headshot taken.

"Well, it's been swell, but I have to go," Emma said. "Like we say in mathletes, be there or B squared."

Augh.

"Bye, Emma!" Tess waved cheerfully.

"Sydney, what are you doing?" I asked her. Sydney was knocking pictures around with her crutch, spreading them out even more.

"Trying to find my headshot," Sydney said. "Yeesh, who *are* all these people?"

"You're making a mess—" I tried to say, but Sydney squealed.

"Squee! There's my headshot! Payton, pick it up off the floor for me since I'm injured?"

I picked up Sydney's model-perfect-of-course headshot and shoved it at her. Then I helped Tess pick up the rest of the pictures while Sydney gazed at her face.

"Oh, I love it," Sydney cooed at her face.

"Tess, you look amazing in yours," I said as I picked up her headshot. She did!

"Thanks!" Tess smiled, picking up the last picture. "Okay, I think we're good."

We all walked slowly down the hall. *Really* slowly, as Sydney hobbled along trying to gaze at her headshot and walk on crutches at the same time. I followed Tess and Sydney into the auditorium.

"There's Nick," Tess said, and we all went toward the front near the stage, where Nick was.

Nick! Okay. Nick. I took a deep breath in through my nose. Then I breathed out through my mouth. That was a trick Emma used when she was nervous about a spelling bee or math competition. Because, yes, seeing Nick made me a little nervous.

It happened after the play and right before the cast party. I kind of sort of figured out that maybe I might kind of like Nick. And that also he might maybe kind of like me. And so I spent the entire cast party turning purple whenever he came by me. Pretty much we didn't say one word to each other.

Yes, I am awkward.

Sydney and Tess sat in the row in front of Nick. I sat down next to them. Okay, I just needed to turn around and say hi. A normal hello like friends would.

"Hiyo," I said.

Nick looked at me funny. I turned back around and faced forward. Hiyo? Did I just say hiyo? I felt my face burning with embarrassment.

"*People!* Your attention, please!" a loud voice boomed out. It was Mrs. Burkle! Our drama teacher. "All eyes on me, please!"

I turned around and put my eyes on Mrs. Burkle. I tried not to think about Nick sitting right behind me. I wondered if he was looking at the back of my head. I hoped my hair wasn't messy. I smoothed it down. It was my best feature and I thought it looked especially shiny since I'd gotten new conditioner. (That I had hidden in my closet to keep it away from Emma, who thought her hair was shinier than mine.)

"When I was a young theatrical ingenue, I had grand dreams of being on Broadway," Mrs. Burkle told us. "However, that was not to be."

Burkle paused and shook her head sadly. Well, that was kind of a downer.

"Mrs. Burkle!" Sydney raised her hand. "But if you had become a star, we would never have had you for a teacher."

I rolled my eyes. Sydney was such a suck-up. It was so obvious to everyone (except teachers and parents, who ate it up).

"Ah, yes, Sydney. Blessings in disguise!" Mrs. Burkle said, perking up. "And now you will benefit even more! My college roommate has made it to the Broadway stage. Well, close. She is the director of an off-Broadway show!"

That was pretty cool. New York City was about five hours away from where we lived. Emma and I had been there once when we were five. I loved all the sparkly lights. Emma had loved counting the windows in the skyscrapers out loud (until our dad had paid her to stop doing it).

I was daydreaming about New York City so I almost missed Mrs. Burkle's major announcement.

"My friend has invited us to see her show. Which means . . . the Dramatic Geckos Club will take a field trip to New York City!"

Tess and I looked at each other. Sydney and I looked at each other. Everyone was silent for a second.

And then there were squeals, screams, and applause! Mrs. Burkle took a bow. And she deserved to!

We were going to New York City!!!!

Emma

Two

AFTER EXTRACURRICULAR ACTIVITIES

Cell phone! My cell phone was ringing with the obnoxious (but #1!) pop song. I reached into pocket number three of my backpack to answer it.

"Hello?" I said.

"Emma, it's me," my twin sister, Payton, said.

Uh-oh.

"I'll call you back! Bye!" I hung up on her.

"Why didn't you tell her?" Ox asked.

We were walking out of mathletes, where we had just gotten some Exciting News. I looked at Ox. (*Ox! The good-looking, popular athlete/mathlete who is—shockingly—my unofficial boyfriend. Unofficial due to* our parents saying we're too young for dating. Which is okay, because we both have academics and activities to concentrate on. . . .)

"Emma?" Ox's voice broke into my thought-babble.

"Oh, sorry," I said. My face was probably bright red from embarrassment. "What did you say?"

"Why did you hang up on Payton without telling her what Coach Babbitt said?" Ox asked again.

"It's just that I have to phrase it carefully," I told him. "Payton is going to be really jealous. She's been wanting to do this for *years*. I just don't want her to feel left behind."

"How sweet," a voice sneered behind me. "Emma thinks she's a Siamese twin, attached to her sister."

I stopped walking and turned around. Jazmine James! My nemesis.

"Miaow," Hector, her evil henchman, said.

"I don't think we're too attached," I said haughtily. "I just care about her feelings. But you wouldn't understand that, Jazmine, since you don't *have* any feelings."

"I have a *feeling* that you're going to *lose* the next mathletes contest . . . to me," Jazmine responded.

"Miaow!" Hector repeated. "Cat fight!"

"Ignore them," Ox advised. So I turned around

and walked down the hallway with him. I could hear Jazmine and Hector following not far behind us. I was so glad Ox was with me. He's not a big fan of the gruesome twosome, either.

My cell phone went off again. As the obnoxious pop ringtone played, I realized suddenly that the tune was not conveying the image of intellectual champion. I reached into pocket number three and answered the call quickly.

"Hey, it's me," said Payton. "I have to tell you . . . I have exciting news!"

Hey. That's my line.

"So do I!" I said.

"I'm going to New York City!" Payton screamed.

Hey. That's my line. Although louder than I'd planned to deliver it.

"Wait, what? *I'm* going to New York City!" I told her. "Are you getting us mixed up?"

"No, you're mixed up," Payton said. "I'm the twin in the Drama Club who's going to see an off-Broadway show in New York City!"

"Well, I'm the twin in the mathletes who is going to a state competition!" I told her. "In New York City!"

"Awesome times two! Woo hoo!" Payton yelled so

loud I thought I'd lose my hearing. In fact, so loud I felt like I could hear her outside the phone.

Ox and I turned the corner toward my locker.

"Where are—" I started to ask, when . . . *wham!*

I crashed smack into Payton. Direct impact.

"Ow!" "Ow!" Our heads banged together. My backpack and Payton's tote bag tangled. One of us slipped, dragging us both down to the floor. We lay in a dazed, twisted heap.

"Oh, I guess they really *are* Siamese twins." Jazmine James looked down on us. "This twin freak show has been entertaining, but let's go, Hector."

Jazmine stepped right over us. Tess, who had apparently been with Payton, untangled our bags. She and Ox helped us to our feet.

"Well, that wasn't too humiliating," Payton grumbled.

"Payton, Emma, are you okay?" Tess asked.

"Do you need ice packs or something?" Ox said. "I can run down to the infirmary and get them."

"No," I said, feeling a little wobbly. "I'm okay."

Ox put his hand gently on my forehead.

He's touching me! Aaah!

"All right," he said. "I'll text you tonight and check on you. If you're sure you're good, I've got to go meet my dad."

"I'll be fine," I told him. "Payton and I are getting picked up too. So we'll be with our mom."

Ox took his hand off my head (sigh), and we all said bye. Then Ox left.

"Emma?" Tess said. "You look a little dizzy."

"She's just swoony with love," Payton said.

"Swoony? There is no such word as 'swoony,'" I said indignantly. *Quick, change the subject.*

"Tess, how are you getting home?" I asked.

"The late bus," Tess said. "Oh! The late bus! I'd better run! You sure you're okay?"

"Yes!"

"We're sure," Payton insisted. "Go! I'll text you later."

After Tess was gone, the hallway was quiet. Payton and I were alone.

"Let's go tell Mom about our trip," Payton said.

Yay! Our trip!

We both started walking to parent pickup. I swung my backpack over my shoulder, but that knocked me off balance and I nudged into my sister.

"Watch out for me! Do you have a vestibular disorder or something?" Payton asked me.

She was joking about the first day of school, when my backpack had hooked onto the door as I was going into science class. And slammed back into the door. Making a scene. Then later in the same class, I'd accidentally tipped my chair back while looking at a poster of Albert Einstein and . . . well, crashing to the floor made another scene. Which caused Jazmine James (nemesis-to-be) to spread a rumor that I had a vestibular (balance) problem. So people erroneously thought I was "dizzy."

"That wasn't funny," I said. "And, uh-oh, neither is that."

I looked at Payton's face.

"Ugh." I winced. "You have a black-and-blue mark on the right side of your forehead."

"Emma," Payton frowned. "You do too."

We both whipped out our minimirrors and groaned.

"We're still identical." Payton sighed.

"Identically injured," I agreed. "But don't worry, I'm sure they will fade by the time we go to . . ."

"New York City!" we both yelled, and headed outside.

When I spotted my mother sitting in our car in the parking lot, I began running ahead. I wanted to beat Payton and be the first one to tell our mom the news.

"Guess what?" I said, breathlessly, jumping into the backseat. "We're going to—"

"New York City!" Payton screamed, flinging herself into the seat next to me.

We buckled ourselves in, talking over each other.

"Off-Broadway!"

"State mathletes!"

"Maybe we'll go see the Fashion District!"

"Or the Financial District!"

Payton did a little dance move in her seat.

"The Empire State Building! The Ferris wheel in Times Square!" she said, shaking her head and pumping her fists.

I was so excited, I started seat dancing too.

I did a (seated) moonwalk on the floor mats.

"Whatever we get to do, it will be awesome, because it's in New York City!" Payton said. "Well, except for your dancing. That's not so awesome anywhere."

I was formulating an appropriately scathing remark when our mother interrupted our NYC fantasizing.

"Girls!" She turned around to look at us. "This all sounds interesting, but first tell me—why are your faces all banged up?"

"Oh yeah," I said, remembering. "Minor collision."

"Totally accidental," Payton said. "Can we have some ice when we get home?"

"And a pain reliever?" I added. "I prefer ibuprofen, but acetaminophen will suffice. Payton, when we get home I want to do a search for the school where they're holding the competition. And find out the previous winners. And—"

"Maybe one of us will be discovered and become a Broadway sensation! As long as it's not Sydney. Gag." Payton gagged.

"I'll have to prepare extra hard if I'm going to destroy Jazmine James and the rest of the mathletes of New York State! I wonder what that T-shirt and trophy will look like? Obviously, totally impressive," I mused out loud.

"Excuse me?" our mother said. "Girls?"

"What?" we both said, still half in our NYC fantasy worlds.

"You've forgotten one little thing," Mom said.

"What?" I repeated, looking at Payton. She shrugged.

"Your parents' permission," our mother stated. "Your father and I will need to have all the information about this trip before we can make a decision."

A decision? Did she mean they might say no?

I received a text. It read *We ARE going. Mills twins in NYC!*

❀ 24 ❀

I texted back, *You and me! NYC!*

It wasn't grammatically correct, but I was pretty certain Payton wouldn't notice.

"Emma? Payton?" Mom said, pulling the car into our driveway. "Stop texting behind my back."

Ulp.

We quickly stuffed our cell phones into our bags and tried to look innocent. Innocent and mature and responsible enough to go to . . .

New York City!!!

E + P = NYC.

Now that's a formula even Payton would like.

Finally we were sitting down at the dinner table. Finally our parents were ready to *discuss* the trip to New York City.

"I checked my e-mail," Dad said, "and I received information from your school along with permission slips. The school will provide transportation. We are responsible for paying for the hotel."

Hotel?

"Hotel?" Payton looked as puzzled as I felt.

"It's an overnight trip," said our father. "Properly chaperoned, of course."

"Sleepover in New York City?" Payton squealed. "Squee! Eeeee! Yay!"

Payton sounded like her usual airhead self, but she also looked even more silly than usual. Our ice machine was broken. So my sister was holding a bag of frozen peas against her forehead.

I couldn't make fun of her, though. I had a bag of frozen corn niblets against mine.

"Mom, Dad," I said. "May we *peas* go on the class trip to New York City?"

"That was *corny*," Payton shot back.

"Okay, Veggie Twins," our mother said, checking under our bags. "It looks like the swelling has gone down."

Whew. Emma and I put down our bags.

"You realize that next weekend is my annual medical-supply conference," our father said.

"Oh!" our mother exclaimed. "I've got a speaking engagement at the science writers conference! The girls would have to go without us."

"There will be other chaperones there," I said.

"And we'll be just a phone call away," my sister reminded them. "Thanks to your generousness of giving us our own cell phones."

"Generosity," I said, correcting her.

"Whatever," Payton said. "The point is that we will be extra good."

"And it *is* a wonderful opportunity for both of us," I added. "May we go?"

Our parents looked at each other. Payton and I looked at each other. It didn't take twin telepathy to know we were both thinking, *Say yes!*

"I'd say it's a yes," our father said, looking at our mom.

"A double yes," our mother said, looking at both of us. And smiling.

"Aaaaaah!" Payton and I screamed, and jumped up from the table. *"We're going to New York City!"*

We danced and jumped around and screamed some more.

"Give me those peas." Mom sighed and held the bag up to her head.

"It's going to be a long two weeks," Dad said, reaching for the bag of corn.

Payton

Three

FRIDAY AFTER SCHOOL IN THE SCHOOL PARKING LOT

"Drama Geckos are in the spotlight!

"Drama Geckos will go far!"

Sydney was calling out a cheer for the Drama Club. We were all standing in front of the bus, waiting to board. It wasn't even a yellow school bus! It was one of those big travel buses with the dark tinted windows!

And it would take us to New! York! City! I was so cheery, I was even enjoying Sydney's cheer.

"Drama Geckos are in the spotlight!

"Drama Geckos are superstars!"

"Okay, now here are the motions we can do with

it," Sydney said. "Split, jump, high V, turn, and finish off with a back handspring!"

Sydney flung herself backward and flipped over.

Uh, I think I'll stick to the yelling and clapping part. This would be an excellent time to start boarding the bus.

"Come on, guys," Sydney said. "Do the motions."

"Are you supposed to do that?" Tess asked her. "Be careful of your ankle."

"Doctor says I'm healed," Sydney said. "So come on."

Tess copied Sydney's jump and arm move thing and threw a back handspring. I stood there.

"Payton, where's your Drama Gecko spirit?" Sydney yelled loudly. "Jump, high V, and back handspring!"

"Sydney, you know we can't all throw back handsprings," I told her. "I can barely do a round-off."

"Ohhh," Sydney said, with a mock sad look. "That's really sad."

She threw another back handspring and cheered loudly.

"Go Drama Geckos!"

Bleh.

"Go Gecko mathletes!" someone yelled back.

A crowd of mathletes were standing in a clump at the other end of the bus.

"Yeah! Gecko mathletes rule!" someone yelled. Oh, great. That was my sister, leading a new cheer.

"Trapezoid, octagon, dodecahedron!

"Bring your A-brains 'cause the competition is *on*!"

Emma's fist pumped above the crowd. Agh.

"Good thing your sister didn't try out for cheerleading either," Sydney muttered to me.

"Oh, Emma would never want to be a cheerleader!" Tess said cheerfully. "When would she have the time? Mathletes, spelling bee. Science Olympiad. Payton, your sister is a true role model."

That *was* true. And I was proud of her. But maybe not at this exact moment, as Emma added an awkward jump and clap.

"Keep trying, math people," Reilly, one of the cutest boys in drama club, snorted. "Drama Geckos rule. Especially since *our* cheers make sense."

We all watched the mathletes cheer. I had to stop Emma. I pulled out my cell phone to text her that.

Brrrzt!

My phone was vibrating. Oh, I had a text message from my mom waiting.

Remember both of your bags! Xoxo Mom

Yup, I'd remembered my bags. I had a little rolling suit-case that was bright green. I was carrying it very carefully because there was something very, very important in it.

My dress!

I was bringing a dress I'd been saving for a special occasion. It was the most beautiful dress I ever owned! It was a Summer Slave dress. This past summer, I'd gone to camp with a bunch of girls who were total fashionistas. One of them was a girl named Ashlynn. She had the cool-est clothes, and she traded me some of them in exchange for doing her bunk chores.

To get this dress, she made me go to the canteen every day and wait in the long line to get her a frozen fruit bar. (Okay, that part wasn't so bad. But she also made me curtsy in front of the whole cabin when I gave it to her. Totally embarrassing, I know, I know!)

But the dress really was worth it.

I also had brought a tote bag with things for the bus:

- ✓ iPod with my new mix
- ✓ Lip gloss (apple flavored, for the Big Apple!)
- ✓ Watermelon gum
- ✓ Water bottle

Mostly I figured I'd be talking with people, though, like Tess! Tess had asked me if I wanted to sit with her on the bus. Definitely.

I was a little worried about Emma. The Drama Club was sitting at the front of the bus. The mathletes were sitting at the back of the bus. Usually on buses I sat with Emma. I hoped she had someone to sit with.

I looked over to check on her. Thankfully, she had stopped cheering. But also . . .

Ooohhhhh!

She was talking to Ox. Ox! Maybe she'd sit with Ox on the bus! That would be so, so sweet. Sharing a bus seat, a love seat, to New York City together.

So romantic!

Ox walked away and Emma stood there smiling. I went over to Emma and squealed.

"What?" Emma said to me.

"You and Ox!" I squealed.

"Yes." Emma sighed happily.

"You and Ox, sharing a seat on the bus to New York City." I clapped my hands. "It's so, so romantic."

"And *so, so* not happening." Emma shook her head and frowned. "I'm sitting with Nima. She's in mathletes."

"Oh," I said. "I'm sorry."

"Sorry for what?" Emma asked. "I asked her to sit with me. This is a *mathletes* competition. Nima aces her conic geometry questions, which as you know, is my weakest section, so she's going to dissect previous years' problems. See how much better that works out?"

Um, no.

"No distractions," Emma said sternly. Then she smiled. "Until maybe after the mathletes competition."

Bus ride home = Emma + Ox! Romance!

"Dramatic Geckos!! Be ready to board!" Mrs. Burkle was yelling.

"Okay!" I said. Then I leaned over and gave Emma a huge hug.

"Even for a Dramatic Gecko, you're being a little overly dramatic," Emma pointed out. "We're going to be on the same bus."

"But still! You'll be in the back with the mathletes. I'll be in the front with the drama crew. We go our separate ways, and then the next time we meet we'll be in New! York! City!"

Emma shook her head as she walked to the mathletes line.

"See you in Manhattan!" I called to her as I went back over to the drama group.

And then we climbed on the bus! It was huge! There were doors in the front and near the back. The seats were high and soft and separate from one another. There were two seats on each side of the aisle.

I followed Tess until she stopped at a row halfway to the back.

"How's this?" she asked me.

"Great!" I said, and Tess sat down in the seat by the window. I stuffed our bags in the overhead above us.

"Here's a seat!" someone across from me said.

Cashmere? Sydney's BFF (best friend/follower).

"Cashmere?" I said. "You're not in Drama Club."

"She is now." Sydney followed behind Cashmere. "She just joined."

"Cashmere, you should try out for the next show," Tess said. "You were so good as the Cat in the Hat in our elementary school play."

I didn't know that Tess and Cashmere went to the same elementary. I also didn't know she starred in a school play.

"Cashmere is a good actress and has a really good singing voice," Tess continued.

"Cashmere is just joining drama to come to New York with me," Sydney explained. "She's not trying out for any plays."

"I don't understand why I can't," Cashmere whined.

I understood. I remembered that Sydney hadn't wanted Cashmere to join drama. It must have been because Sydney wanted to be the star! She was afraid of the competition!

"Save our seats," Sydney snapped at her. She tried to lift her giant suitcase.

"Oh, there's Nick. He can help me with my bags."

Nick came down the aisle. He helped Sydney put her two huge chocolate brown and pink suitcases into the overhead compartment. Then she slid into the seat with her stuffed tote bag on her lap.

"Whew! That's a lot of stuff!" he said.

"Nick to the rescue," Sydney said. "My hero!"

Gag.

But I couldn't say anything. I could barely look at him! Nick stopped next to where Tess and I were sitting.

"Hey, guys," he said.

I blushed and looked down.

It's not like I wanted to avoid Nick. I just didn't know what to say! I couldn't believe it. I used to make fun of Emma for not being able to talk to boys. And now I was the one turning purple.

"Is anyone sitting here?" he asked, pointing to the seat in front of us.

"Where's Reilly?" Sydney asked. "Reilly might want to sit there."

Nick was cute. But Reilly was definitely the hottest guy in drama. He was in eighth grade and didn't seem into Sydney, but that didn't seem to stop her from trying.

"Reilly's already sitting up front." Nick pointed to the front of the bus. "So I guess it's cool if I sit here."

He slid into the seat in front of me. Tess poked me. Yay! I could stare at the back of Nick's head for the whole trip!

"Dude!" A guy named Charlie came down the aisle and stopped at Nick's seat. "I'm sitting with you."

"Sorry, Sam's already planning on it," Nick said.

"Not anymore," Charlie said cheerfully. "Burkle is making us change seats. She doesn't want me sitting with Reilly because we're trouble with a capital *T*."

"Go tell Burkle to let Reilly sit here instead of you," Sydney told him.

"*Pht*, I'm not going up there." Charlie shook his head. "It's all teachers. Besides, Burkle told Reilly she needed to keep an eye on him. She blames him for the eighth-grade campout bus spitball incident last month."

We all leaned to look. Sure enough, Reilly was sitting next to Mrs. Burkle. He was going to have a *loooong* trip!

Coach Babbitt called for the mathletes to get on the bus from the back door.

"The back seats are so much cooler." I sighed. "Why do the math geeks get to sit in the back?"

And at exactly the same time, someone behind me said, "Why do the drama geeks get to sit in the front?"

It was Emma! In class, Emma always likes to sit in the front seat, close to the teacher. I guess the bus was the same.

I turned around and climbed onto my knees to see what was going on. And looked right into the face of . . .

Emma!

She was sliding into the seat right behind me.

"Oh, hello," Emma said to me. "I guess you didn't need to say that whole dramatic good-bye."

"I didn't think you'd sit right behind me," I said. "I thought we'd be separated."

"You can pretend I'm not here," Emma said.

I slid back into my own seat.

"Cool," Tess said. "We can all hang out!"

"What is the total surface area of a right circular cone

with radius five and altitude twelve?" Emma said in a not-quiet-enough voice.

Ergh. Annoying. I turned around and leaned over the seat. Emma was droning on.

"Emma!" I said. "Are you going to talk math to yourself the whole trip?"

"No," Emma said.

Phew.

"I'm going to talk to Nima, remember?" Emma said. "This is Nima." A girl with long dark hair sat down next to Emma.

"Hi, Nima," I said.

"Acccck!" Nima looked up and shrieked. Emma and I jumped at the same time.

"Are you okay?" Emma and I said at the same time.

"There's two Emmas?" Nima said, still looking startled.

"Oh, I'm her twin," I said, reassuring her. "You haven't seen us in school? Or maybe . . . on the school VOGcast?"

"Nima can be a little oblivious to the world," Emma said. "Right, Nima? That's why I like her. She's focused. All math, all the time!"

Nima smiled like she'd been given a compliment.

"Sorry I screamed," Nima said to me. "I thought I

was seeing double. Maybe I'd been studying multiplication so much, even people multiplied."

"We look alike but we're totally different people," I started to say. But Emma turned to Nima.

"Emma," Nima said, "the answer to your conic geometry question—which is my specialty—is ninety times pi."

All right, enough of that. I slid back into my seat. Their chanting math problems floated around and wedged in my skull.

"Okay, they are going to drive me crazy," I said to Tess.

"Mathletes competitions are pretty intense," Tess said. "Practicing is a good idea for the trip."

Oh yeah, Tess used to be on mathletes too.

"A gelato shop has four different flavors and six different mix-ins. If you wanted to get one flavor and two different mix-ins, how many different combinations could you get?"

I just couldn't tune her out! And then Tess called out, "Sixty."

"That's right!" Emma said. "Good job, Tess."

Oh no! Tess was going to get sucked in too.

"Uh, Emma?" I leaned over. "Would it be possible

for you to switch seats and go sit somewhere else? Pretty please?"

"The front seat is a sign of academic power," Emma explained. "The front seat in class, the front row of the bus. Sitting here gives me a mental edge going into the competition."

Then she lowered her voice.

"And Jazmine James has the other 'front' seat," she whispered. "So I can't give her the win."

I looked over across the aisle. Jazmine James was sitting in her seat with Hector. They were quizzing each other too.

Well, I didn't want those two sitting behind me either. It was like the rectangle of evil over there, with Sydney, Jazmine, Hector, and Cashmere.

Defeated, I slid back in my seat. I'd have to ignore the goings-on behind me, but at least I could look at Nick's head in front of me.

"Help," I pleaded to Tess. "Entertain me so I don't have to hear Emma's voice."

"Do you want to do math problems?" Tess asked. "I could quiz you."

"*No!*"

"I'm kidding!" Tess said.

"Children! Children! Please direct your attention to the back of the bus."

We all turned around to see a woman in a black suit and red scarf standing in the aisle near the back. When Jazmine groaned, I realized it was her mother.

"I am Mrs. James. I am one of your parent chaperones." Mrs. James looked stern. "We are seated in the very back of the bus, if you need our assistance. Or to go to the restroom, which also is located in the back of the bus."

Everyone was like, "Ewww! Go to the bathroom on the bus? No way!"

I noticed Jazmine had shrunk down in her seat and looked embarrassed. It made me very glad that my parents were not chaperoning.

"Students! Please remain seated while the bus is in motion!" Coach Babbitt announced.

And then the bus started to move. We were off!

Tess and I drew pictures on our hands with markers. We talked about our favorite songs and the show that was on last night. We talked about wizards versus werewolves versus fairies. Then I played Tess my new ringtones on my cell.

"Do you want some snacks?" Tess asked. She pulled out her tote bag.

"I hear snacks!" A head popped over the top of the seat.

"Swedish fish." Tess held up a bag.

"Yum," Charlie said. He reached over and grabbed a handful.

"I have cheese puffs," I said. "They're in my overhead case."

I got up and stood in the aisle. I reached up and found the cheese puffs where my mom had packed them in the outside pocket.

I could see Nick sitting in the seat in front of me. And he looked up and smiled at me.

Ah. He had a cute smile. I tugged on the bag of cheese puffs. Then my suitcase tilted and started falling on my head. Whoa! I pushed it back and then—

"Hey!" I heard my sister yell.

And Nima yelped and Tess gasped and Charlie started laughing, because cheese puffs were falling from the overhead!

"Dude, cheese puffs from the sky!" Charlie tried to catch them in his mouth.

"Sorry! Sorry!" I said.

Emma stood up to help me and grabbed the cheese puffs bag just as it fell completely. Unfortunately, that just poofed the remaining cheese dust into the air.

"Hey, look." Charlie laughed. "Orange twins!"

I looked at Emma. She had massive cheese-puff fall-out in her hair. I'm sure I matched. I saw Sydney and Cashmere laughing hysterically. I couldn't even look at Nick.

Could this be any more embarrassing?

"Excuse me," Emma said, looking to Charlie. "The proper term is 'conjoined twins.' And Payton and I were never conjoined. But the most famous pair were Chang and Eng, who were conjoined at the liver and traveled with a circus."

Yes. Yes, it could be more embarrassing.

"Maybe you two could travel with the circus," Sydney suggested.

"Emma, why don't you help dust off Nima?" I said brightly. "And shush."

"People!" Mrs. Burkle's voice rang out. "Emma Mills, are you standing? Even though I stated everyone must stay seated while the bus is in motion? Are you breaking my rules?"

"Mrs. Burkle, I was just . . . I was just . . . ," Emma called back frantically. "I was just about to suggest a bus singalong! For . . . Gecko spirit!"

A what?

"A Gecko singalong!" Mrs. Burkle said happily. "What a marvelous idea! Emma, why don't you lead us in song!"

"Me?" Emma said, turning deep purple. She looked at me for help. Sorry, singing was one place twin-switching would not make a difference. Neither of us could sing.

Emma was frozen.

"Sing." Sydney smiled. And then I thought of someone who would sing.

"Cashmere!" I said. "Do you know 'Three Cheers for the Bus Driver'?"

"Duh," Cashmere said, and started singing. Whew! And wow! She did have a good voice. No wonder Sydney wouldn't let her try out.

"Everybody sing!" Mrs. Burkle joined in. Coach Babbitt's voice boomed.

"Three cheers for the bus driver, best of them all!"

Everyone was singing. Well, pretty much everyone. I was mouthing the words. I was sure Emma was too.

Phew.

Brrrrzt. Emma was texting me.

Thx for the save!

I texted her back.

? What were u thinking? U wanted 2 sing?

I choked! I couldn't think!

Well, every1 is ☺ now.

Except me. It's too loud to practice math.

Gee, I felt so sorry for her. Not! I did feel sorry for *me.* I had totally embarrassed myself in front of Nick. I leaned over to pick up some cheese puffs as everyone switched to singing a Barney the dinosaur song and cracked themselves up.

I tried to wipe the orange off my fingers.

"Here." Emma handed me something through the seats. Hand wipes. Of course. Emma always carried a pack of them.

"You can use them up," Emma said. "I brought a travel two-pack. And just so you know, if you need bandages, floss, or duct tape, I came prepared."

Four

STILL ON THE BUS

"New. York. *City!!!*"

I looked up from my mathletes book. People were cheering. I stood up to look over at Payton. Some moments I needed to share with my twin. I knew she was as excited as I was to be in the city.

Payton was asleep, her head tilted back against the seat.

"Payton!" I said. "We're here!"

"Oz?" Payton asked. Oh, she was sleep-talking. Heh.

"Wake up, Payton!" I said. "Tess, shake her a little. Otherwise she'll sleep through the whole trip."

"Trip? Click your heels three times," Payton said, eyes still closed.

Tess grinned and shook Payton awake.

"Wha?" Payton asked, a piece of hair sticking out at a thirty-degree angle from her head.

"Good morning, bedhead," I said to her. "Technically bus head."

Payton patted her hair, felt the wayward chunk, and said "Gah!"

I smiled and sat back down in my seat, where Nima still had her nose in her math book. I looked over her and saw tall buildings in the distance. Not like *our* hometown tall. Skyscraper tall! Our bus was crossing a bridge over the Hudson River that led to . . .

"New York City!" Everyone started cheering. I looked over at Jazmine James. She was staring down at her study book, ignoring the noise.

"Mathletes! Dramatic Geckos! Silence!" Coach Babbitt didn't have much volume, but his voice meant *no nonsense.*

Silence.

"The seat across from Mrs. Burkle is currently unoccupied," Coach Babbitt said. "Someone needs to return to his or her seat immediately. No wandering."

"It is Samuel!" Mrs. Burkle said, and raised her voice. "Sam the munchkin! Return to your seat immediately!"

I remembered Sam, from the *Wizard of Oz* play.

"Maybe he went back to Munchkinland?" Hector suggested loudly.

Jazmine snickered, but she did not move her eyes from the page.

"Boy, she's really serious about this competition," I whispered to Nima.

"She wants to take back what is rightfully hers," Nima whispered to me. "The mathletes championship."

Excuse me?

"That championship is rightfully mine," I said, louder than I'd intended. "I won."

"Only because I had caught a virus from your snotty twin rugrats," Jazmine said.

By "rugrats" she meant Mason and Jason. Okay, they kind of sneezed on her.

"You'd better keep studying, then," I said in my best competition voice.

"So should we," said Nima. "We've got approximately fifteen minutes before our arrival in Times Square. Emma, how many points with integer coordinates are exactly five units away from the origin?"

I pictured the coordinate plane and calculated using the distance formula. "Twelve points," I said.

❀ 48 ❀

"Correct." Nima nodded.

"Sam the munchkin!" Mrs. Burkle yelled again. "Yoohoo! Are you in the restroom? You're taking a long time! We're waiting for you!"

Lots of people giggled.

"Ox!" a voice hissed. "Hey, Ox!"

Yikes!

The voice came from under my feet! Then Sam's face appeared from under the seats ahead of me.

"Aaack!" I shrieked.

"Aaaack!" Nima shrieked.

"Where's Ox?" Sam said, looking up at us.

"Not under our seat," I told him.

"Why are you crawling on the floor?" Nima asked. "How can you even fit under there?"

"Didn't you hear?" Hector said, blurting in from his seat on the other side. "He's a munchkin."

Jazmine snorted.

"I couldn't take it up there anymore. Burkle's been doing some vocal exercises. She sounds like she's a gargling cat."

Payton's and Tess's heads popped over their seat backs.

"Sam," Payton complained, "you're kicking my legs."

That made sense. They had the lower part of Sam's body under their row.

"Oopsie," Tess said, and dropped a chunk of bagel. It bounced off Sam's head.

"Hey!" Sam exclaimed. Loudly.

"What is going on here?" Coach Babbitt came down the aisle and stopped at our row.

"Emma Mills is harboring a fugitive," Jazmine James said.

"I am not." I glared at her. "He just . . . appeared."

"Sam, get up," Coach Babbitt ordered.

"I think I'm stuck," Sam said, his face turning a shade of red.

The bus was quiet. Everyone was interested now.

"Who knew all the drama would be in the mathletes section?" someone in front of us said. *Ha-ha.*

Then.

Thump. Roll. Thump. Roll. A strange sound grew louder and closer, then *bump!*

"Ow!" Sam yelled. "Something just hit me."

Tess disappeared, and then came up holding a soda can.

"It must have rolled down from the front," Tess said.

Nima and I pulled our legs up onto our seats to

give Coach Babbitt room to reach down and assist Sam. Coach Babbitt tugged, and Sam slid out.

"Back to your seat, Sam," Coach said. "We'll discuss your consequences up there." Coach Babbitt went back up the aisle. Sam calmly stood up, brushed himself off, and moved to the aisle.

Whew. I stretched my legs out.

"Thanks," Sam said. I was about to say "You're welcome" when I realized he was talking to Tess. He'd taken the soda pop out of her hand.

"All that crawling made me thirsty," Sam said.

Oh. No.

"Don't—" I was going to explain the scientific results of rapid molecular movement and a sudden release of energy when it happened.

Sam popped the top.

Ka-floom! Foam, bubbles, and liquid exploded into the air. And then gravity intervened, and it all rained down. Mostly onto the two people on the inside aisle. Payton and me.

First we were cheesed.

Now we were soaked.

"At least it's clear soda," Tess said, trying to console us. "It could have been much worse."

"This is bad enough," Payton said grimly, trying to shake droplets out of her hair.

"We're twin targets for disaster," I said.

"Man, I'm gonna get in double trouble," Sam groaned. Then he ran back up the aisle to this seat.

"I hope Mrs. Burkle tortures him for the rest of the trip," Payton grumbled.

"Here." I reached into inner zip pocket number two of my travel bag and pulled out one of my emergency "magic cloths" for my twin.

"Soaks up any spill in under ten seconds," I said. Payton said thanks, and she and Tess vanished from view. I used my backup emergency cloth (inner zip number three) and dabbed at my hair, shirt, and jeans.

"Ten . . . nine . . . eight . . ." Nima and I counted down the seconds.

"How cute," Jazmine said. "They're practicing counting backward." Hector laughed.

"Two . . . one!" I checked my clothes. Hey, not bad. The magic cloth absorbed almost all the soda pop. *What a relief!*

"Excuse me, people," Coach Babbitt said loudly. "Quiet, please. We need to go over the rules. Every one of you will be representing our school in New York City.

You must uphold the Gecko rules of safety . . ."

Coach went over the sheet of rules we had all received with our permission slips. I turned and looked out the window. Tall buildings, taxicabs weaving in and out of traffic, and an incalculable number of people everywhere.

Oh, yeah. This was it! Soon we would park and disembark and split up—those drama people off to do their acting stuff, and mathletes off to do mathletic and other *important* activities.

"As Geckos, we will all be supporting one another this weekend," Coach Babbitt was saying. "This means that our mathletes will not only attend the play with the drama club but will also be going backstage at the theater."

"A once-in-a-lifetime opportunity!" Mrs. Burkle exclaimed in a voice that could put a gecko in a coma. "A cultural and artistic treat for our Geckos!"

"What?" I said. "But we need to focus on what's important here: Math!"

The back of the bus muttered "Yeah!" and "Math!"

Payton leaned around her seat and shushed at me.

"And that also means that our Dramatic Geckos will be attending a mathematics lecture and also cheering on our mathletes at their tournament," Mrs. Burkle announced.

The front of the bus made groaning sounds.

It was my turn to shush Payton, who was saying "Sheesh!" and "Ugh!"

"*Bo*-ring," Sydney whined loudly from her seat across from my sister. "We have to waste our time in New York doing geeky math stuff?"

Waste our time?

Geeky?

I chose to ignore Sydney, who was ignorant about the important things in life. Which, at the moment, was the math book in my lap.

Math > zero >Sydney.

Time to get some last-minute studying in.

Payton

Five

TIMES SQUARE, NYC!

I pressed my face to the window. I could see blinking lights! Huge signs advertising random things! Zillions of people walking around everywhere!

Times Square! I had to share this exciting moment with my sister. I turned around and leaned over my seat.

"Emma!" I said. "Times Square!"

Emma barely looked up from her math book.

"Did you know Times Square is known as the Crossroads of the World? It's a major intersection of the blocks at Broadway and Seventh Avenue," she mumbled.

Oh, dear.

"Hm, if it spans the blocks between Sixth and Eighth,"

Emma said, "and West Fortieth and West Fifty-third. That would mean the perimeter of the square equals . . ."

"Emma!" I interrupted her. "Stop being a math robot for just a minute and look out your window! It's *Times Square!*"

"Big whoop," Sydney said, nearly hitting me on the head as she pulled her bag from the overhead. "We went to New Year's Eve here and watched the ball drop from our hotel room. We were so close, people probably thought I was a celebrity."

"This is so cool," Nick said.

"Thank you!" I blurted out. "Finally someone appreciates it!"

Nick leaned around the seat.

"I've never been here before," he said.

"Emma and I haven't been here since we were little," I replied.

"It looks crazy out there," Nick said.

"I know!" I agreed.

Then he smiled at me. I smiled back. We were having a conversation! A normal conversation like before, when I thought he might be a good match for Emma and didn't like him. *Like* him like him. And before I heard he might like me. If he still liked me.

"People!" Burkle announced. "I will assign you to a parent chaperone as you disembark the bus."

"Maybe we'll be in the same group," Nick said to me.

Eep! I got a stupid grin on my face but I didn't have time to answer because the line in the aisle started moving.

Everyone started pushing up the aisle to get off the bus. I grabbed my bags and stood in the aisle behind Tess. Emma got up and stood behind me, reading her flash cards.

"Why are these people pushing?" Emma grumbled behind me. "They might bend my flash cards."

"Emma." I turned around. "We're in New York City. Take one minute to stop thinking about math and appreciate this!"

"Fine." Emma sighed. "It's Times Square! We're in New York City!!!"

We both grinned at each other.

"Six point zero five," Jazmine said loudly from her seat. "Am I right, Hecky?"

"You're right!" Hector said.

Emma stopped grinning at me.

"Okay, the minute is up," Emma said. Her nose went back into her flash cards.

I tried. The line started moving forward.

"I hope we're in the same group!" Tess said.

"I hope, I hope, I hope," I agreed.

We inched up the aisle until Tess was in front of Mrs. Burkle.

"Tess! My Dorothy! Your chaperone is Mrs. Nicely," Mrs. Burkle said as she scanned her list. Then she looked at me.

"And you are with . . ."

I held my breath as Mrs. Burkle scanned her list for my name.

"Mills, Mills, oh, there you are," she said. "You're also with Mrs. Nicely."

Yessss!

"Yay, Payton!" Tess said happily. She held her hand up for a high five.

"Oh, wait, you're Payton?" Mrs. Burkle frowned. "I mixed that up. *Emma* is with Mrs. Nicely."

Tess dropped her hand. I ended up awkwardly swiping empty air. "Oh, bummer. Well, I haven't hung out with Emma in a while," Tess said. "And, Payton, I'm sure you'll have a fun group."

"Payton, you're with Mrs. James," Mrs. Burkle said. "Jazmine's mother."

Noooo!

"Can't I just switch with Emma?" I asked Burkle.

"You want to switch with your sister?" Burkle asked me.

"Yes!" I said happily. "You can go back to pretending you thought I was Emma like you first did."

Burkle frowned at me.

"There will be no switching! Do not even *think* about asking me about switching!"

I turned beet red as everyone looked at me. I hurried down the bus steps and saw Jazmine's mother with her hand in the air.

"Well, at least we'll share a hotel room," Tess reminded me.

True. We had put each other on the "who I want to room with" questionnaire. I waved good-bye to her and went over to Mrs. James. I must have been the first person in the group.

"And you are?" Mrs. James peered at me.

"Payton Mills," I told her. "Emma's sister."

"Emma who?" Mrs. James looked at me blankly.

I would have thought she'd know Emma. Jazmine only had been competing against my sister forever. And last time, Emma had beaten her daughter. Oh. I suddenly realized who Jazmine had learned her mind games from.

"Uh, never mind," I said. I shifted away from Mrs. James.

Anyway, there were better things to think about. I was in *Times Square*! There were huge, flashing signs on the sides of the buildings. And the buildings were so ginormous! There were bright lights blinking. Tons of people walking everywhere. It was crazy!

I craned my neck to look up at the tall skyscrapers. Then I looked at the blinking ads. Whoa. I felt a little dizzy. I stumbled back.

"Stay away from the curb," Mrs. James said sternly.

I wasn't even near the curb! But I stepped even closer to the buildings, anyway.

"Sorry," I said. "The signs made me a little dizzy."

"They're called *spectaculars*," Mrs. James said. "The largest ones are called JumboTrons."

"Oh," I said. "Gotcha."

I stood awkwardly and watched other people join their groups. People were squealing and hugging one another. Tess was standing by Mrs. Nicely. And there was Emma, joining her. And there was Nick joining them.

Nooo! Emma got to be with Tess and Nick!

I got to be with . . .

No no no no no. Sydney was walking our way. No no no no.

Sydney stopped and rolled her eyes at me. Then she turned to Jazmine's mom.

"Hello, Mrs. James," she said in her Tricking Grown-ups About My Evilness voice. "I'm Sydney Fish. It's so nice to meet you."

Mrs. James held out her hand. Sydney reached out and shook it.

"Not a handshake," Mrs. James said. "Spit."

"Excuse me?" Sydney asked her.

"No gum chewing," Mrs. James said sternly, and held her hand under Sydney's face. "Spit your gum out *now*."

Sydney looked pained but also intimidated. Then she spit out her gum into Mrs. James's hand. Ewwww! Mrs. James went to a trash can and tossed it.

"Okay, that was disgusting," Sydney said.

"Seriously," I agreed.

"Oh, you're here," Sydney said, pretending to notice me. "This isn't our whole group, is it?"

I hoped not. Then I changed my mind. Jazmine was walking toward us, reluctantly.

"There you are," Mrs. James said.

"I can't believe I'm with my mother," Jazmine muttered.

"Your mother, who heard you mutter that, requested you specifically," Mrs. James said to her. "To ensure you are using time wisely. Did you finish listening to your math downloads? And complete the worksheets I drew up?"

"Yes, mother," Jazmine said.

I actually felt bad for Jazmine. I shot her a sympathetic glance.

"What's your issue?" Jazmine said to me. "Stare much?"

Okay, I didn't feel so bad anymore. So great, it was me, Sydney, Jazmine, and her mother?

"Hey, we're in this group." Reilly and Sam came up to us.

"Yay, Reilly's in our group!" Sydney said, and started hanging all over him.

"And me!" Sam whined.

"And the munchkin," Sydney said.

"Group," Mrs. James said. "Here are the rules. Later on we will head to the hotel to check in to our rooms, but until then, we will explore Times Square."

"Yes!" Sam said, and started to move.

"Halt!" Mrs. James said loudly and scarily. "Boy who needs a comb, stay with the group."

"Sorry. Also, I spilled soda on my head, so that's why I'm extra spiky," Sam explained, patting his spiky hair. "And sticky."

"We will all be sticky. As in, stuck together as a group," Mrs. James said. "For safety purposes, you also will each have a buddy."

"My buddy!" Sydney pulled on Reilly.

That left me with Jazmine or Sam. Jazmine sighed. I sighed. I started to walk over to Jazmine. And then she stood next to Sam.

"Fine, I'll be with Munchkin," Jazmine said.

She picked him? And that left me with . . .

"Then you're with me." Mrs. James pointed at me.

Um, what?!

"You will stick with your buddy at all times," Mrs. James said. "March in a straight line."

This was so not good. I was the parent chaperone's buddy? I had no choice but to follow Mrs. James down the block.

"Ew, we don't have to hold hands," Jazmine said to Sam. "This isn't kindergarten buddies."

"You can hold my hand," Sydney cooed to Reilly.

"No handholding!" snapped Mrs. James. "Behave."

We walked quickly to the next street.

"Excuse me, where are we going first?" Sydney asked Mrs. James.

"A very important institution," Mrs. James said. Ooh! What would we see? We crossed a street and stood in front of a gray building.

"This is one of the world's largest financial institutions," Mrs. James said.

Um. Okay?

We stood there and stared at it.

"We're staring at a bank?" Sydney whispered to Reilly.

"This will gear you up for the math competition," Mrs. James announced. "Thinking of large numbers and financial figures! Focus, focus, focus!"

"Mrs. James?" Sydney said. "Most of us are here for Drama Club. Jazmine is the only mathlete."

"Hm," Mrs. James said. "Is there a drama competition?"

"No," I said. "We're here to see a show."

"Then have your priorities straight!" Mrs. James said. "Competition trumps passive watching. Now, we have one hour and much to do. Follow me."

We silently followed her to the green space in the middle of Times Square. Last time I'd been to New York there had been cars and taxis everywhere, but now it was full of people sitting in chairs set up near a stage.

"Sit," Mrs. James said. She stood in front of us and started to lecture. About math! She was teaching us math! And not any math, but mathletes math, that only Jazmine and Emma and maybe Tess would know.

Everyone except Jazmine sat looking at Mrs. James, totally confused.

Bbbzt!

My cell! I reached into my pocket and sneaked a look. It was from Emma.

Ridiculous. We are in a candy store with world's biggest chocolate bar. Everyone's eating candy. People are running around crazy on sugar and stealing my flash cards.

What? They were in a chocolate store? And I was listening to a math lecture?

P: *Trade places w me! ;-)*

E: *NO*

P: *Bring me chocolate?*

E: *Too late. We're going somewhere else. Hopefully somewhere quiet.*

Sigh. So. Mrs. James was talking about mathletes

stuff. Blah blah blah. I turned to see another group going by laughing and having all kinds of fun times. This was lame. I was in Times Square! And listening to a math lecture for geniuses?

E: *UGH! Now we're in toy store. Too loud to study. Tess and Nick are riding little-kid bikes around. Ugh! Emma*

What? They were in a toy store? That was *so* not fair. I looked across the street and could see the toy store. It was huge! And inside, Tess was with Nick, having fun.

And then all of a sudden it started to rain.

"Eek!" Sydney said. "My hair!"

"It's just a sprinkle," Mrs. James said. "Fresh air is good for children. You are wearing slickers. Put your hoods up or put your umbrella up."

Ugh. I pulled up the hood on my jacket. And stood in the rain.

"This is ridiculous," Sydney grumbled as the rain came down more.

"Ladies? Want to share my umbrella?" Sam asked. "Cuddle close."

We all inched away from him. A car drove by and splashed water on my feet. I'd had enough! Then I had a genius idea related to mathletes. Okay, not involving math but . . .

"Mrs. James," I said, "I'm concerned that if we stay out here any longer, someone will catch a cold."

Mrs. James looked at us.

"You don't want Jazmine to catch a cold before mathletes competition?" I said. "Again?"

"Oh. Yes, that is a good point," Mrs. James said. "Everyone head inside to the—"

Before she could say bank or who knows what boring math building, I spoke up.

"To the toy store!!" I yelled. "Let's go!"

Six

GINORMOUS TOY STORE

I stood in line with Nick and Tess. For a kiddie *Ferris wheel*. Mrs. Nicely, our chaperone, had blindsided me. I figured a librarian would take us to the New York Public Library or a literary equivalent. Where I could study among the books. But Mrs. Nicely said we were here for "fun!" And "toy shopping for her grandchildren!" So here we were.

"This is a waste of time," I muttered. It was infuriating. Sure, I had been happy when I'd heard we were going to New York City. But we were going for a math competition, not a vacation! "I . . . have to go to the bathroom."

"Hurry up, we're almost there!" Tess called as I

headed away from the wheel. I was a little afraid of heights. Standing behind a stack of stuffed animals, I began calculating that height plus too many rotations would equal . . . me being sick to my stomach."

"Aaah!" A wet, slickered person jumped in front of me, waving! I'd thought Times Square wasn't dangerous anymore, but some people were obviously acting a little crazy.

"*Shhh!*" The Slicker faced me, and inside the hood was Payton!

"What the heck are you doing?" I whispered. "You freaked me out."

"No time to freak," Payton said. She was whipping off her rain slicker. "Time to switch."

What?

"Here, put this on," Payton said. "You're me. I'm you. You know the drill. Here. Behind the stuffed animals where no one can see us."

"You heard Mrs. Burkle," I said. "No switching." I looked around for our people. I saw no chaperones or students.

"Emma, we have to switch," Payton said. "If I have to listen to Jazmine James's mother's math tips for another second I'm going to . . ."

Twin say what?

Did I hear that correctly? Math tips?

"She keeps going on and on with tips and competition advice." Payton nodded. "Nobody except Jazmine cares."

I cared! Oh, I cared!

"Give me that." I grabbed Payton's slicker. I pulled it over my head. "Where's Mrs. James?"

"At the entrance." Payton pointed to Jazmine and her mother standing near the front door looking bewildered.

"Bye, Emma!" I said in my twin's cheery voice. Yes, I was no longer Emma, as far as the world was concerned. As far as Mrs. James was concerned.

"Hello, Mrs. James," I said, making sure my Emma outfit was covered by the slicker.

"Payton!" Mrs. James exclaimed. "What were you thinking running off like that? And into a toy store?"

Jazmine smirked at me. I thought fast.

"I just wanted to get out of the rain." I said, "And I thought that being here would—erm—show you how frivolous other groups were and we'd be motivated to study with you."

Jazmine looked at me a little harder. Oops. Payton would not use the word "frivolous."

"At least that's what Emma said when I told her I wanted to come here," I kept going. "She said toy stores were frivolous and . . . um . . . childish."

"They most certainly are," Mrs. James said. She pointed at Sydney, Reilly, and Munchkin. They were goofing around nearby.

"Well, I'm not going anywhere in this rain," Jazmine announced. She set her tote down on a table demonstrating some toys.

"We will have to do our competition training right here." Mrs. James sighed and sat down next to her daughter.

"Ooooh!" Mrs. James squealed and jumped up.

"Squeeee!" A toy pig flipped in the air and tumbled off the display table.

Mrs. James had sat on a pig. It was really hard to stifle a laugh. I distracted myself by leaning down and picking up the pig and putting it on the other end of the table.

"Well," Jazmine's mother huffed and sat back down. "Jazmine, I will give you a number and you tell me if it is divisible by three, six, seven, or some of those, or none."

"Wait." Jazmine frowned and looked at me. "Why is *she* still here? Don't you want to go play, *Payton*?"

"Uh," I said Paytonly. "I need to sit for a few minutes. These shoes are sooo cute, but not so good for running in the rain."

I sat down near the James.

"Ignore me," I said. "I—er—won't understand or anything. Visible by what?"

"*Di*-visible." Jazmine rolled her eyes.

A group of little kids wielding foam swords began fighting in front of us.

"Hi-ya!"

"I got you, Jake! You're so dead!"

"Children!" Mrs. James said. Her voice made the kids freeze. "Take your fight elsewhere! Shoo!"

The kids fled. Mrs. James could be seriously scary. I, however, was not intimidated. I needed to get her back on math. And not that simple divisibility stuff. I needed some more-complex tricks.

"Um . . ." I cleared my throat. "I remember Emma saying how great Jazmine was in game . . . something. I see all the games here in the store, and it reminded me how"—I coughed—"jealous Emma was about how good Jazmine was at that."

"She means game theory," Jazmine said. "And it's true, I am so superior in that area."

I wanted to throw up. Complimenting Jazmine felt faker than pretending I was Payton. But it worked. Jazmine and her mother worked aloud on advanced game theory, and since everyone's math brain works differently I was able to learn some new methods. Until some people our age wearing crazy hats started playing with the flipping pig. Loudly.

While Jazmine and her mother tried to get rid of them, I looked back up at the Ferris wheel. Twintuition! I saw Payton sitting in a little car with a cartoon character on it. She was with Nick.

They were both sitting close to each other. Payton and Nick! Nick and Payton! Oh, yay!

Oh, wait!

Oh no! Payton was supposed to "be" Emma! Nick might think I *like* liked him! Twin telepathy time!!!!

Payton! I aimed my thoughts at the Ferris wheel. *You are Emma! Do not flirt with Nick in public! Repeat. Do not flirt—*

I heard a giggle. Ugh. Sydney was back with the other two boys in the group.

"Reilly, you were such a rock star on that video game," Sydney was gushing. Speaking of flirting . . .

"Hey, Payton." Sydney's voice had turned even more

sticky-sweet. "Isn't that your twin on the Ferris wheel with Nick? They look pretty cozy."

"Gah," I choked out. *Alert! Payton! Twin telepathy, activate!!!*

"Does this mean Ox finally got a clue and dumped Emma?" Sydney went on. "Or is she—*gasp!*—two-timing Ox behind his back?"

"Pretend" Emma's and Nick's car circled into sight again. They were both laughing.

Twin telepathy fail.

"Seems like Emma's more into boys than math these days," Jazmine chimed in. "She won't stay competition material much longer."

"That's right, Jazmine," Mrs. James said. "Good thing we raised you better than that."

"Wait . . . it's not . . . I'm not . . ." I couldn't figure out how to defend myself, when I wasn't supposed to be me.

Sydney and Jazmine and Mrs. James were staring at me. I felt like a bug trapped under an electron microscope. Mean girls! Mean mother! Aah! What would Payton do?

No clue. I fled. Toward Payton and Nick and the Ferris wheel. I needed to save my reputation. Fast.

Seven

HIGH UP IN THE AIR

Doo dee doo. La la la. Hee hee hee.

Okay, yes. I am on a Ferris wheel with Nick. In the middle of a toy store, in New York City, I am on a Ferris wheel with Nick.

Squee!

At first it was confusing when everyone mixed up me and Emma. And then how I got pushed into the group with Tess and Nick. And how Tess and I were at the front of the line.

"Tess," I'd whispered. "It's me! Not Emma! I have to go and switch back—"

And that's when she interrupted me.

"I think I'll skip this ride. Nick, can you go on with Emma?"

"That's not Emma," Nick said, puzzled. "Hey, Payton."

And then Tess had shoved us together and onto the Ferris wheel ride!

Squee!

"I love Ferris wheels," he said, as the car moved slowly up. "Don't you?"

Actually, I was a little freaked-out. The Ferris wheel was kind of tall, and then when I looked down I could see everyone looking up at us. And all the giant toys and statues in the store.

And sitting next to Nick.

Squee!

Eeek! I looked down. I could see people running all over. I squinted and tried to see Emma. I thought I could see her in my raincoat, surrounded by what looked like people with foam swords running around.

Ooh boy, we were at the top of the wheel. I was feeling dizzy. I decided to look at Nick again. He was smiling.

Squee!

"How's your group going?" he asked me.

I decided to sort of shut my eyes and ignore the fact that I was dangling in the sky.

"Ergh," I said. "Mrs. James is trying to teach us math the whole time."

"I'm glad you got to take a fun break," Nick said. Then he looked at me closer. "Are you closing your eyes? You *are* having fun, right?"

"Yes," I squeaked.

"You're a little green," Nick said. "You're not going to puke are you?"

No! *No* I will not puke on the Ferris wheel with Nick!

"Definitely not," I squeaked. But I shut my eyes more.

"Well, the bus ride was long and bumpy," Nick said. "I can see why you might get Ferris-wheel sick after that."

I nodded. I didn't trust myself to open my mouth to speak in case something else came out.

"Hang in there," Nick said. "I'm sure it won't be much longer."

Up. Down. Around.

I wished this would end. Why couldn't I be sitting next to Nick somewhere not a zillion feet in the sky, turning round and round?

❀ 77 ❀

I clenched my lips tighter. Then I felt something around my shoulders. What was it? I opened my eyes. It was Nick's arm! It was Nick's arm around my shoulders! The feelings of pukishness suddenly disappeared. And I felt happy.

It almost seemed like I was on a date. A super-romantic date! High on a Ferris wheel in New York City.

Squee!

"Is this helping?" Nick asked me. "I thought pressing your shoulders down would make you feel grounded so you wouldn't throw up."

My happy feeling disappeared. He was trying to stop me from puking. This was not romantic. I frowned.

"Uh-oh," Nick said. "I guess that didn't help. Sorry."

He whipped his arm off me.

"No," I tried to explain. But the Ferris wheel car swung as he moved his arms. I clamped my lips shut.

"I didn't mean to be awkward," Nick said. "I thought it might help."

Agh! He was totally misunderstanding! I wanted his arm around me! But not because he thought I might puke!

I was on an emotional roller coaster. No, an emotional Ferris wheel.

And then the wheel reached the bottom. It was our turn to get off. Nick helped me stagger off the wheel. Tess came running up to us.

"How was your ride?" Tess asked, smiling.

"Whew," Nick said. "I'm so glad that's over."

Glad it's over?

Tess looked at me and stopped smiling.

"I—" I tried to say something but suddenly someone grabbed me by the arm. I assumed it was Emma, but I could barely see her face since she had my raincoat hood pulled tight.

"Come," she said, tugging at me.

"But—" I tried to turn back to Nick and Tess.

"Emma!" Emma gave me a look. *"Come!"*

Then she yanked my arm and dragged me away.

"Go back to your group!" Emma said. "We're about to get busted. I will *not* get in trouble and get thrown out of the math competition just so you can have a romantic carnival ride."

"Where's my group?" I asked her.

Emma dragged me through a crowd of people.

"But I need to tell you something!" And I needed to go back and talk to Nick. And it definitely was not a romantic carnival ride. But it was too noisy. "Tell Nick—"

"There you are!" a voice boomed behind us. We turned around to see Mrs. James and the rest of my group.

"Payton." Mrs. James frowned, looking back and forth at us, not sure who was who. "As my buddy you are to be with me at all times. Do *not* run off again. Emma, do you know where your group is?"

"At the Ferris wheel," Emma and I both said at the same time.

"Then join them," Mrs. James commanded.

I made a signal to Emma that I'd text her what happened. Then I joined my original group—Jazmine, Sydney, Reilly, and Sam—as they followed Mrs. James as she practically knocked small children over on her way out the door.

And I saw Emma as she hurried over to Nick and Tess and the rest of her group. I so wished I could run over there. I just needed a minute to explain. Or to fix things with Nick. Actually, what I needed was a do-over of the whole time with Nick!

But not on the Ferris wheel. Somewhere on the ground that didn't move.

We followed Mrs. James out the door and onto the street in front of the store.

"Yay, it's not raining anymore," Sydney said. "Can

❀ 80 ❀

we go to the makeup store across the street so they can fix my makeup?"

"Absolutely not!" Mrs. James said. "I am unhappy—and I repeat, *un*happy—with the behavior shown in the store. There has been a breach of rules."

Oh no! Mrs. James knows I left the group! She knows I went on the Ferris wheel! But it wasn't my fault!

"It was an accident!" I blurted out. "Totally harmless!"

"Harmless?" Mrs. James looked sternly at me. "Someone could have been injured!"

Huh?

"They were just foam swords," Reilly said. "They didn't hurt or anything."

"I was aiming for Reilly," Sam said to Mrs. James, looking guilty. "I didn't know your daughter was going to jump in front of me."

Mrs. James was glaring at the boys.

Oh, phew, it wasn't me.

"You hit my daughter in the face with the sword," Mrs. James said. "And right before a math competition."

Sydney giggled. Jazmine glared at her.

"What? It was a little funny," Sydney said.

"Not funny," Jazmine said.

"You need a sense of humor," Sydney whispered so Jazmine could hear her.

"You need an IQ," Jazmine shot back.

Yeeps. I edged away from that, um, discussion, and closer to Mrs. James. I relaxed a little bit knowing our switch hadn't been busted.

"Our hour is coming to a close," Mrs. James was saying. "We are to proceed to our next destination, where we will meet up with the rest of your classmates."

No more math lessons? Aw, too bad so sad.

"However, it is several blocks away, so we will continue our math lessons as we walk," Mrs. James said. "Coordinate geometry or logarithmic equations?"

"Logarithmic equations!" Jazmine said.

The rest of us groaned. We walked in a group across the street.

"Find the logarithm of the ninth root of three," Mrs. James ordered.

"Hmm . . . ," Jasmine said. "It's definitely a fraction. One-fourth?"

"Oh, this is painful," Sydney said. "Look at what we're missing. Shopping. Fun restaurants. A TV station!"

"Sports restaurants!" Reilly added. "Sports-stuff stores!"

"Comic stores," Sam said miserably. "Candy stores."

We all sighed as we passed a candy store.

"We're probably going to a math store next," Reilly said.

We marched along in silence. I tried to keep up and not get run over by the crowds pushing along the sidewalk. Or trip over other tourists who were pulling rolling suitcases.

"Hey, Payton," Sydney said.

Or walk near Sydney. I walked even faster.

Sydney caught up easily. "Look, there's another group over there." I could see some of our classmates on the other side of the street, with one of the dad chaperones in the geeky Gecko cap.

"So?" I asked.

"There's Ox," Sydney said. "Do you think he knows? Somebody's definitely going to tell him. Do you think he's going to get really upset? Do you think he's going to go punch Nick out?"

What the heck was she talking about?

"No, he won't punch Nick out," she continued. "Emma's not worth it."

"Sydney, what are you talking about?" I asked her.

"Duh, how your sister, Emma, was cuddling up with

Nick on the Ferris wheel?" Sydney said. "How he had his arm around her? I know Emma and Ox aren't officially boyfriend and girlfriend but—"

"*Augh!*" I yelled out. Oh my gosh! Oh my gosh omigosh omigosh! I had not even thought of that! People saw me and Nick on the Ferris wheel except . . .

I was supposed to be Emma!

"And aren't you so mad at her too?" Sydney went on. "It's pretty obvious you had a crush on Nick. And now your very own twin sister is stealing him."

"No!" I blurted. "That's not what's happening! It wasn't—"

"You're in denial," Sydney sighed. "It *is* shocking. I mean, who would have thought your brainiac geek of a sister was such a guy magnet?"

Okay, okay. How was I going to explain this one? Maybe I should just tell her it was me. I mean, the whole thing was an accident.

But how could I prove that? And after the mix-up switch-up, we should have told a teacher or something. Sydney could totally use this to get us in trouble. Or she'd hold it over my head so I would be worrying that she could tell on us at any time.

I was so confused. Plus feeling kind of dizzy and

pukey still from the Ferris wheel. I needed to text Emma. She would know what to do. I pulled my phone out of my bag. I realized it was turned off so I clicked it on.

"We are here!" Mrs. James announced.

Emma

Eight

SIDEWALKS OF NYC

"New York, New York!" Tess sang out, raising her hands to the skies. Which were drizzling rain down on us as we walked along the sidewalk.

My mood felt like the weather. Dismal.

"You've got a great voice," said one of the eighth graders in my group. I didn't know her.

"Thanks." Tess blushed. She looked at me and Nick. Neither of us had said much since leaving the toy store.

"Emma! Nick! Cheer up! We're in the Big Apple!"

"Big Apple?" Mrs. Nicely turned back to check on us. "Did I hear the mention of food? Good timing, I say, because our next stop is the pretzel stand on the corner ahead."

"Pretzels, yay," I said, attempting to sound enthusiastic.

"Pretzels, yum," Nick said, sounding suspiciously like me.

"Sheesh!" Tess sighed. "I don't know what's wrong with you two, but if you don't snap out of it soon, I'm hanging out with . . . excuse me, what's all you guys' names again?"

"Katelyn."

"Adam."

"Russ."

The three eighth graders slowed down to join us.

"Yeah," Tess repeated. "I'm hanging out with Katelyn, Adam, and Russ. What are we talking about?"

"We're quizzing each other on factorization and common multiples," Adam said. "You wouldn't understand."

"Tess was the winner of last year's mathathon," Nick informed them.

"And you chose drama over math?" Katelyn frowned.

"Ugh," Adam said. Russ nodded. The three of them sped up and left us behind.

"Drama versus mathletes?" Tess said, loudly and

dramatically. "We're all Geckos! Can't we just get along?!?"

Okay. Even I had to smile at that.

A few minutes later we were sitting around some modern statue eating steaming pretzels in paper wrappings. Mrs. Nicely was on a nearby bench, surrounded by bags from the toy store. We all had our slickers on and hoods up.

"Will somebody *please* tell me what is going on?" Tess demanded, taking a bite of pretzel.

"It's nothing," Nick said. "I just thought . . . well, I totally misunderstood a situation." Nick did not look at either of us. He looked—sad.

Maybe if *I* talked about the Ferris wheel deal, I could figure out why.

"So," I began, "here's *my* problem."

"If it's math-related, I can't help you," Nick said. He had yellow mustard on his cheek. I did not get the pretzel/mustard combination, but whatever.

"No," I sighed. "You're actually part of the problem. You two know that Payton and I switched places by accident, right?"

They both nodded. Boy, it was weird to be talking about twin switching with someone other than Payton, but Tess and Nick had told me they'd known we'd traded places right away.

Which was why Nick had looked so cozy with my twin on the Ferris wheel.

Wait. Shouldn't Nick be in a good mood after that ride with Payton?

"When I *accidentally* got stuck in Payton's group, Sydney noticed . . ." my voice trailed off. Sydney noticed what? I had *thought* Sydney and everybody had noticed Payton and Nick acting like they like *liked* each other. Like more than just friends.

But now that Nick was acting weird, what was I going to say? *Sydney's telling people that it was I, Emma, who was flirting with Nick, instead of Payton, and she is going to make sure Ox finds out about it, when really it was Payton and Nick who were so happy on the Ferris wheel together . . .*

But Nick didn't seem so happy now. This was way too confusing. If this were a math equation, it would be like $(N + P) - (N + E) + (E + O) + (S + O) = (E - O) + (P - N)$.

"Sydney noticed what?" Tess broke into my over-thinking. "That you two switched places! Oh no, is she going to tell on you? Like Jazmine did when she busted you two the first time?"

"No, that's not what Sydney's going to blab . . . ," I started to say, but got cut off by a shriek from Mrs. Nicely.

"Children!" she said, jumping up. "We are due at the theater in exactly six minutes! Where did the time go?" She grabbed all her bags and took off at a brisk walk.

I noticed one of the mathletes (Russ?) check his GPS and announce: "We have eleven blocks to go. That's one point eight three blocks per minute. Time equals distance divided by rate."

"We'll make it in time if we hurry," Katelyn(?) said. "Taking into account variables like the traffic signals and taxi aggression."

Reality check! Those people already had their math brains churning, while I was once again distracted by personal problems.

"Let's go," I sighed, dropping my wrapper in my backpack until I could properly dispose of it. I had eaten the whole pretzel without even noticing.

Tess, Nick, and I caught up with the rest of our group and headed full speed toward the theater. By the time we were finally there, I was out of breath—I'm a mathlete, not an athlete—and had put Nick's grouchy face, Payton's problems, and all evil nemeses (a.k.a. Sydney and Jazmine) out of my head.

Ox I'd deal with later.

Now it was back to the me I should be. Mathlete Emma. Focused Emma. Academma.

"Hi, Payton!" a drama Gecko said to me as we joined another group at the theater entrance.

I was too winded to correct her. By the time I'd caught my breath, I was inside the theater and following Mrs. Nicely to our seats.

"Please turn off all electronic devices," our chaperone announced, reading from a sign on the wall.

My cell phone! I'd completely forgotten about it. Quickly I pulled it out of pocket number three and texted Payton. *Find me!* I punched in the message fourteen times so she would understand the urgency. I shut my phone down and slipped it back into its proper pocket. No one had noticed.

Whew.

I flopped down into a theater seat. I looked around for my twin's group. They weren't here yet. Good. Then Payton would still be outside and receive my text. Texts.

Gah. This was just too much drama for an elite mathlete like me. I closed my eyes and began calculating the products of my favorite prime numbers.

Nine

OFF-BROADWAY THEATER

"We are here!" Mrs. James had announced.

Where was here? I looked up from my phone. We were at a theater! I could see the sign for the play that Burkle's friend was going to produce!

"A real Broadway theater!" I said.

"Off-Broadway," Mrs. James sniffed. "Off-off-Broadway."

Still! It was so cool! It wasn't that far off Broadway for one thing!

Brzzzzt! Brzzzzt!

My cell phone started going crazy and interrupted me. I looked down to see fourteen text messages. Fourteen? I clicked and saw they were all from Emma!

?!?!?!

"Cell phones off!" Mrs. James said to me. "Immediately! No cell phones in the theater."

"But—"

She glared at me until I turned it off. We all filed into the theater. And I forgot about my cell phone.

"I call front row!" Sydney squealed, and darted down to the front.

"Group! Be seated," Mrs. James said. We all followed her to the front row. I tried to go slowly but somehow I ended up stuck between Sydney and Jazmine James.

But now I would ignore them! I was in a real Broadway theater! And who knew? Maybe I'd be an actress on a stage like that someday!

My dreams were interrupted by an elbow in my waist.

"There's Ox," Sydney said in a singsong voice.

I saw our classmates start to enter in groups.

"There's Nick! There's your twin sister," Sydney said. "All the people in the love triangle. Oh, and you! A love square! Let the drama begin!"

"Speaking of drama, why do the mathletes have to do this?" Jazmine whined to her mother.

"Unfortunately, your coach thinks this is a valuable

cultural experience, even with your competition tomorrow," Mrs. James said with a sniff.

People started sitting in the rows behind us. I tried to turn around to see Nick or Emma or Tess. I spotted Emma.

She held her hand up in our "twin, check your text" signal. I shook my head and tilted it toward Mrs. James. My twin telepathy worked! She frowned and then shrugged. Emma sat down next to Tess.

And on the other side of Tess sat Nick. I tried to wave at him, but he was talking to Tess. I wasn't even sure if he would wave back, anyway.

"Ladies and gentlemen!" I turned back around as Mrs. Burkle came onto the stage. "Dramatic and Mathletic Geckos!"

Everyone quieted down, except Reilly, who let out a "Wooot!"

"Welcome to the theater!" Burkle said. "It is quiet now, but soon it will be filled with the sounds of glorious music and theater in the new show: *Fairytale Mash-up*! And I'm proud to say that this play is produced by my dear friend—Jane!"

Everyone clapped as a woman with black hair pulled back in a bun came out onstage. She was wearing a black dress over black tights and spiky high heels.

Glamorous!

"We are thrilled to have the students of my dahlink Bertha Burkle with us today!" Jane said. "Hello, dahlinks!"

"Bertha?" Sam snorted.

"Producing my new play, *Fairytale Mash-up*, is a dream come true!" Jane said. "I remember when I had the seed of the idea: What if the stories of *Cinderella*, *Beauty and the Beast*, *Alice in Wonderland*, and *Snow White* were mixed up together?"

Everyone was like, Ooh! Cool!

"You will have the privilege of seeing our show premiere tomorrow," Jane continued. "But we have a special treat for you today."

"Treat, shmeet. I can't believe we have to use our math competition study time for this little play," Jazmine sniffed, just like her mother.

"A show this close to Broadway in New York City is *not* a little play," Sydney said, leaning over me and putting her hand on her hip. "This is a big deal."

I could actually agree with Sydney for a change.

"Yeah," I said to Jasmine. "We get to go behind the scenes and see how the show is made. We might even get to meet the actors!"

Maybe even the stars!!!

"And now . . . for a special appearance: introducing the stars of *Fairytale Mash-up!*"

We all were like, Yeah!! Woot!

"That's so cool!" Sydney squealed. "The stars!"

"Our leading lady, Zoe-Marguerite!" Jane announced.

A woman came out onstage and blew kisses to the audience. We clapped and clapped.

"Our leading man, who will be playing Prince Charming, Rohan!" Jane said.

"And last, but not least, introducing our ingenue," Jane said, "a talented young lady who is soon to be a star!"

We clapped as a girl with blond hair walked out onstage and curtsied. And blew kisses. And—

Ashlynn . . . Ashlynn? *Ashlynn!* From my bunk at summer camp? From New York City? *She* was the star of the show we were seeing? The girl who called me Summer Slave all summer as I did chores in exchange for her clothes? The clothes I was *wearing right now*?

Oh no. I scrunched down in my seat. I covered up my face—and my super-cute black T-shirt with the sparkles, which I had gotten after a day of scrubbing Ashlynn's muddy sneakers.

She couldn't see me, right? And even if she did, she

couldn't recognize me, right? Right? I pulled my hair over my face just in case. I crossed my arms over my Summer Slave shirt.

"What is your issue?" Sydney whispered to me.

I didn't respond. I didn't want any attention called to us. Especially me. I scrunched down even farther in my seat.

I so could not believe this. Jazmine James on my left. Sydney on my right. And in front of me, onstage, as my classmates cheered her on . . .

Ashlynn from summer camp.

Ten

ANOTHER PART OF THE THEATER

Ashlynn?

Ashlynn from summer camp? Ashlynn, who worked on her tan while Payton worked for her in exchange for overpriced, albeit sometimes cute clothing.

I looked over at Payton to see if she had figured it out yet. Oh yes, there she was. I could see her, but only barely, since she was scrunched down hiding the fact that she was wearing The Star's hand-me-downs.

Okay, it's not funny.

No, it *is* funny.

Ha.

HAHAHAHAHA

HAHAHAHAHA
HAHAHAHAHA
HAHAHAHAHA
HAHAHAHAHA
HAHAHAHAHA
HAHAHAHAHA
HAHAHAHAHA
HAHAHAHAHA
HAHAHAHAHA
HAHAHAHAHA
HAHAHAHAHA
HAHAHAHAHA
HAHAHAHAHA
HAHAHAHAHA
HAHAHAHAHA

Eleven

STILL IN THE THEATER

"That Ashlynn is gorgeous," Sydney sighed. "And look, she's wearing the new TC Couture skirt that isn't even in stores yet!"

"She's sooo cool," Sydney breathed next to me.

"She's not so cool," I muttered.

I was having flashbacks of how cool she wasn't—at least to me. Ashlynn laughing as I did her bunk chores. Ashlynn naming our bunk "Ashlynn and The Fash-lynn's Plus Payton." Because, she explained, I couldn't qualify as a "fashlynn" since I had no "fash."

That's when I started doing chores for her clothes. Oh sure, everyone in my bunk knew I was getting her hand-me-downs. But nobody in my new middle school would know that, and it would be worth the suffering.

"Hello, hello, children," Ashlynn said dramatically, while standing in the spotlight on an almost-Broadway stage.

Children?!! Oh, please. She was my age. In fact, she was two months younger than I was.

And that's when I heard a noise coming from the back of the theater.

GAK! GAK! GAK!

"Is someone choking?" Mrs. James whispered.

Everyone started turning around to see what it was. Except me, because I knew what it was. It was Emma laughing. Well, not exactly laughing, but it was the noise she made when she was trying not to laugh. Of course, Emma must have been trying not to laugh because she recognized Ashlynn. Emma always thought it was funny/slightly insane how I let myself be treated by Ashlynn.

Oh no! Ashlynn! Ashlynn, onstage, stopped talking and started looking out into the audience too.

Shhhh! Emma! Don't let Ashlynn spot you!

Phew, my twin telepathy must have worked because the choke-laughing stopped. I could not believe I was squished between Jazmine on my left, Sydney on my right, with Ashlynn in front of me and my twin making disturbing noises behind me!

This was an NYC nightmare!

"As I was *saying,*" Ashlynn said loudly, "your Drama Club teacher asked me to do an acting exercise with you."

"Excuse me!" Jazmine raised her hand. "Excuse me!"

"Yes?" Ashlynn looked over our way. I scrunched down again.

"We're not all Drama Club students," Jazmine said. "Many of us have an important mathletes competition. Perhaps our time would be better served if we left now to go study."

Jazmine started to stand up.

"Sit down, Ms. James!" Mrs. Burkle's voice boomed. "This cultural experience is valuable for all Geckos. You will remain."

Jazmine sighed and sat back down.

"Ha-ha," Sydney sang under her breath.

"I'll share a theater exercise I learned in my exclusive acting class with world-renowned acting coach Harriet Greenspan," Ashlynn said. "Hm, I will need some volunteers to assist me."

I could not have slumped down any farther without being under my seat.

"First, the girl who already volunteered," Ashlynn said. She pointed at Jazmine.

"What?" Jazmine sputtered. "I didn't volunteer."

"Jazmine James, go onstage!" Burkle's voice boomed out.

Jazmine scowled and went up the aisle to the stage.

"Me!" Sydney started waving her hand. "Me! Me!"

Hopefully, Ashlynn would pick Sydney, and then I'd be free of both of them.

"Definitely the boy in the blue shirt." Ashlynn smiled. She pointed at Reilly.

"Oooooooh" Sam and some other guys started making kissy noises. Reilly stood up and flexed his arms.

"And the boy in the brown." She pointed at Ox.

"That's okay, I'm here with math club, not drama." He shook his head.

"Oh, you're definitely leading-man material," Ashlynn cooed. "Come on up."

Ergh. I sneaked a look back at Emma. She was frowning. Yeah, Ashlynn's not so funny anymore is she, Emma?

"She's picking the hotties," Sydney grumbled.

"And I need another girl . . ." Ashlynn looked around.

"*Me!*" Sydney waved her hand. "Over here!"

"Over there . . . ," Ashlynn said. "Okay, girl in the black shirt."

"I'm wearing floral." Sydney looked confused.

But I was wearing black. I tried to see if Ashlynn was just randomly calling me, or if she recognized me, while at the same time pretending not to hear her. La la la. Just pick someone else.

"Girl in the cute black with the rhinestones!" Ashlynn said.

"Oh, ick, she means you," Sydney said to me.

"Go up instead of me," I muttered. "Go ahead. Now's your chance."

"If you say so." Sydney shrugged. She got up and stepped over me into the aisle. Unfortunately, the aisle was blocked by Mrs. Burkle.

"Payton!" Mrs. Burkle said. "Your time to shine! Go on up on that stage and show your stuff!"

This had potential to be a disaster. I turned around to catch Emma's eye. She gave me a look. My twin telepathy could tell she was sending me sympathy thoughts for the embarrassment and humilation that was to come.

I went up onstage. Stay calm, Payton. Stay calm.

"Hey," I said as I walked past Ashlynn.

"Hello," she said.

She didn't recognize me! She didn't recognize me! It must be because I look so much different now. At summer camp I was tanner and, well, the showers were gross so I often wore a ponytail.

Wheeeewwww!

I quickly went to the end of the line of people, as far away from Ashlynn as possible. That left me next to Ox, who looked really uncomfortable.

"You don't look too happy about this," I whispered to Ox. "Me either."

"But you like acting," he whispered back. "Hopefully she'll just ask me a challenging math question and I'll be done."

I looked out into the crowd. Everyone was looking at me, Ox, Reilly, and Jazmine onstage. Well, probably everyone was looking at Ashlynn. Especially the guys.

"Time for some improv!" Ashlynn announced. "I'll assign each of my actors a role and a scene. And when I say go, you will interact with each other based on the role."

"You, girl in the yellow?" Ashlynn said. "You are a witch."

"Excuse me?" Jazmine glared at her.

"The Evil Witch," Ashlynn said. "Don't take it personally. Remember? It's a fairy-tale mash-up. Zoe-Marguerite, our star, plays the witch."

Jazmine looked slightly less mad. But still suspicious.

"You could be one of the three little pigs," Ashlynn said. Everyone cracked up.

"Witch is fine." Jazmine gave her the death glare again. I thought that was a good look for her character.

Reilly was Prince Charming.

Ashlynn told Ox he was the Beast, from *Beauty and the Beast*.

"Not that you're beastly," she pointed out. "But you're big and strong."

Good thing I couldn't see Emma's face for that one!

"And you." Ashlynn came over and stood in front of me. "You are a servant girl."

Hey. And wait. A servant girl? I looked closely at Ashlynn, but she smiled back kindly.

"In the play, the servant girl turns into Cinderella," Ashlynn told the audience.

Okay, that made sense. I guess it was just random that she assigned me that. At least I'd end up a princess.

"However, that's later. Now you're just a servant girl doing the bidding of the queen," Ashlynn continued.

"The rest of the story is yours to make up. Ready? Go!"

Ashlynn went to the side of the stage to watch. Okay, I needed to be a servant girl. I hunched down and pretended to be scrubbing the floor.

Reilly went up to Ox. "Beast, I have a terrible task ahead of me. I need your help. I need to find my true love and slay dragons. Will you help me, Beast?"

"Sure," Ox-Beast said. "Why not."

"And now I need to find my true love! My beautiful princess!" Reilly announced dramatically. "Is that you?"

He stood in front of Jazmine. Jazmine was staring at her cell phone.

"I said, is that you?" Reilly asked again.

"Ew, no. And can you take this elsewhere?" Jazmine said, annoyed. "I'm studying Pythagorean triples on my math app."

"Cut!" Ashlynn swept out onstage. "You are breaking character! You never want to break character!"

Jazmine glared at her, looking like she wanted to break something, but not character. Hee.

"Put away the math, Ms. James," Burkle called out from the audience.

Jazmine stuck her phone back into her pocket as Ashlynn went to the side of the stage again.

"Fine," Jazmine huffed. "I'm the Evil Witch. I am going to . . . uh . . . poison you."

"No, no!" Reilly exclaimed, and put his hand to his forehead. "Do not poison me!"

"Servant Girl, bring me a poisoned apple," Jazmine announced. "Hurry up."

I went over and pretended to hand her something.

"Cut!" Ashlynn said. "Okay, audience, tell me what the problem is here."

Everyone was silent.

"Look at the Servant Girl," Ashlynn prompted. "Does it look like she's holding a poisoned apple?"

"No!" Sydney called out, raising her hand. "Unless it's the size of a grape."

Everyone cracked up. I turned red. Then I widened my hand to the size of an apple.

"And how about her characterization?" Ashlynn asked. "Is she believable? Is this how a servant girl would approach a queen?"

Ergh.

"When you're in character, what you really need to do is think about how your character walks, talks, and stands. Get into their head."

Everyone was nodding.

"Let's practice, Servant Girl," Ashlynn said. "Wouldn't you, say, get down on your hands and knees and look subservient?"

Fine. I got down on my knees and held up the "apple."

"For example, the Servant Girl should look beaten-down. Imagine her in old rags. All dirty and smelly. Imagine her wearing old secondhand hand-me-down clothes." *Secondhand, hand-me-down* clothes.

And she grinned at me.

And that's when I realized: She knew it was me.

She knew it was me.

Twelve

STILL IN THE THEATER

Payton and I have this list of Top Ten Stupid Questions People Ask. Number five is *When someone punches your twin, do you feel her pain?*

The obvious answer is "No, of course not."

But a new question has occurred to me. *When someone humiliates your twin, do you feel her pain?*

Answer: Yes. Especially when it is onstage in front of an audience made up of your classmates.

"Huh," I heard Sydney say, way too loudly. "No wonder the star didn't choose me. Her actress instinct told her Payton Mills would be perfect as a loser slave."

For the first time in recent memory, I did not stop

to think before I reacted. Or should I say, *acted* before I thought.

"Halt!" I stood up in the audience and projected my voice as if I were confidently answering a math question. (Which I would be tomorrow, so this was good practice.)

"What?" Ashlynn turned to look out into the audience seats.

"I said 'halt,'" I repeated, climbing over Tess into the aisle and walking toward the stage. I climbed up the steps and faced the Evil Witch Jazmine.

"Hey, you can't just come up here!" Ashlynn protested.

"Audience participation improvisation!" Mrs. Burkle clapped her hands in delight. "Wonderful twist to the story!"

"Uh, here." Jazmine "grabbed" the poisoned apple from my twin sister's hand and stiffly held it out to me. "Eat it."

"No one will eat that apple!" Ox suddenly leaped in and took the invisible fruit from Jazmine and pretended to throw it far off the stage.

Wow. As quarterback on our school's football team, Ox really knew how to fake throw.

"Who are you supposed to be?" Payton asked me.

"I . . . I am you, Servant Girl. You of the future," I stuttered. "I've come to tell you that you will become Cinderella and get your Prince Charming and live happily ever after! Just—er—hang in there and don't let the haters get you down."

Okay. That didn't sound remotely like me. Perhaps *I* was getting into character. Maybe I was a natural actress after all!

"Beautiful vision of the future," Ox said to me. "Tell me, will I always be this horrible beast?"

At that moment I became aware that I had just interrupted a play in progress and that I was a person with stage fright. And that Ox was so handsome.

"Nurggh . . . ," I said. And froze. I looked at Payton, hoping she would see the panic in my eyes.

"Oh, thank you, future me!" Payton said, standing up. "Now I know I will someday soon defeat the Evil Witch"—she dismissed Jazmine with a wave—"and become a princess!"

"There she is!" Reilly shouted. "My princess!" He headed toward Payton.

"I will escort you to the future," Ox said in a fake-Beast voice. He took my arm and led me behind the curtain backstage.

"Cut! I mean, stop!" Ashlynn shouted. "That is *not* how this was supposed to go."

"Aah, that is the beauty of improvisation," I heard Mrs. Burkle squeal. "One *nevah* knows what will happen in live *theatah*!"

Ox and I looked at each other and cracked up. Quietly.

"That was something," Ox said, shaking his head. "It's never boring with you twins around."

"Is that a bad thing?" I sighed with relief as I sat on a prop chair.

"Well, I know what's a good thing," Ox said. "Getting to spend a little time with you."

I knew my face had just turned bright red. I smiled. I didn't know what to say. I heard Ashlynn order a new group onto the stage. Then I heard Sydney's voice. She was all gushy because she had been assigned the role of Good Fairy. Figured. Sydney had a way of getting what she wanted. Except for Ox, of course.

Ox!

Sydney!

"Ox, I need to tell you something!" I said in a rush. "Sydney is spreading a rumor that I like Nick because everyone thought they saw the two of us on the Ferris wheel close together!"

"You and Nick?" Ox frowned. "Why would they think that?"

"Uh." I knew I had to be honest with Ox. "It *looked* like me, but it was really Payton pretending to be me."

Ox's eyes opened wide. *His greenish-brown eyes with little flecks of gold . . .*

"You switched places again?"

. . . that have frowning eyebrows above them.

"Well, yes, but it was an accident," I said, "and it was only for a brief time."

Silence.

"We didn't do it on purpose! It was totally a mix-up!" I insisted.

"I believe you," Ox said. *Whew.* Then he said, "So what are you going to do to fix it?"

Oh.

Out on the stage there was silence. Then Nima's voice yelled, "Unhand me, you evil dwarf!"

Then Sam's voice complained, "Why do I always have to play the short character?"

"Emma?" Ox said.

"Okay," I said, deciding. "I'll just tell Sydney and everyone that it was Payton and not me," I said. There. All fixed.

"But didn't you two promise the school you wouldn't switch anymore?" Ox raised one eyebrow.

Huh. I didn't know he could do that. It's cute. He's so cute . . .

"Uh, yes," I admitted. I needed a loophole. "But we're not *at* school. So it doesn't count?"

"I don't know." Ox frowned. "It's a school-sponsored trip."

"Well," I sighed. "I will just have to accept my punishment."

What would it be? Detention? Or worse . . . suspension? Or . . .

"Ox, what if they kick me off mathletes?" I wailed.

"Emma, I— " Ox started to say.

"Announcement!" Coach Babbitt's voice boomed. "All mathletes form a group right here."

Ox jumped up.

"The drama stuff must be over," he said. "Come on, we don't want them to think we're missing."

I followed him out.

"What were you"—huff, puff—"going to say . . ." I tried to ask Ox about his saying "Emma, I—" but his legs were so long, I could barely keep up with him. Within moments we had blended into the mass of mathletes standing under a glowing exit sign.

"Listen up, mathletes," Coach Babbitt said. "While the Drama Club continues their dramatic activities, we will be walking over to auditorium seven, where the competition will be held tomorrow, for a practice."

"Yeah!"

"Awesome!"

We were all excited. Finally! Math! Plus I'd get another chance to talk to Ox.

I searched the area for the Drama Club and Payton. I didn't see them. They were probably taking a tour or something. Hopefully Ashlynn had left the building and gone back to her penthouse condo or mansion for good.

It had been funny to see the Payton-Ashlynn reunion, but I didn't want my twin to be tortured for too long. Just a little. (Hee.)

"As our venue has separate locker rooms for the males and females," Coach continued, "boys will come with me. Girls, you'll go with Mrs. James."

What? No! I needed to talk more to Ox! I waved and signaled at him, trying to get his attention, but he was looking the other way.

"Twin!" Mrs. James's voice barked in my ear. "Stop fidgeting and stay by me. You and your sister are obviously double-trouble-makers. Honestly, I do not know why the school allowed you two to take this trip."

Ouch.

We all started walking. There weren't that many girl mathletes: Nima, three eight graders who stuck to themselves, Jazmine, and me.

The competition arena was just a few blocks away. But when we'd left the building and were out on the sidewalk, the boys' group was nowhere in sight.

I sighed.

"Emma, what's the matter?" Jazmine sidled up to me and spoke in a low voice. "Can't handle being away from both of your boyfriends? Of course, as soon as they find out you're two-timing them they'll dump you. What a distraction. It is going to be so hard to concentrate on math."

"I do not have two boyfriends," I said through gritted teeth. "I do not even want *one* boyfriend. I am focused, Jazmine, and I am going to squash you like a bug."

"Mother!" Jazmine called. "I thought you were going to keep the twin near you. I fear she is plotting some more shenanigans."

I groaned and moved a little closer to Mrs. James. I put on my competition academma face and tried to block out all emotions. I ignored Jazmine's smirk. I avoided looking up at the tall buildings. I matched my breathing with my walking, staring straight ahead.

Now, that's focus, I scoffed inside my head. I was steady, calm, and determined. I was a winner. I was tripping. I was falling. I was on my face on the sidewalk, with Jazmine's black boot near my nose.

"Oops!" I heard Jazmine say. "Emma has vestibular issues, you know."

"I do not . . . ," I sputtered, pulling myself up. Nothing felt hurt. Except my pride.

"Yes, she loses her balance a lot," Nima added. "Remember that day in science class . . . ?"

"I'm okay," I said loudly. "Thank you for asking."

"Well, then, let's keep moving, people," Mrs. James said. "We don't need any more distractions. It is almost time for mathematics."

"Yay!" everyone cheered.

I cheered the loudest, to show Jazmine I was just fine. I channeled Payton and was all spirity and excitable. My twin might be the actress, but I would perform like a champion once the mathletics competition began.

Thirteen

BACKSTAGE

"You did a great job onstage, Payton," Tess said to me as we stood in line.

That wasn't acting. That was real life! Let's see, I had to bow down and be a servant to Ashlynn from summer camp. And act scared of her. And look beaten-down. And act like I was wearing secondhand clothes.

Yup, it was just like real life.

Although, now I'd have to really start acting. The mathletes had all gone off to do their math thing. And the Drama Club people were in line for something everyone thought was so exciting:

Getting Ashlynn's autograph.

I obviously did not want Ashlynn's autograph.

"I'm so thrilled to meet her," Sydney said.

A part of me wanted to say "I lived with her for the summer."

That would impress Sydney and Cashmere for about three seconds. Then they would want to know why Ashlynn and I hadn't acknowledged each other onstage. And why I was hiding from her now.

I decided I'd fake a huge sneezing fit right before it was my turn. I'd have to run off and if I got dragged back, I'd tell them I didn't want to get my germs on the star.

I didn't want to see Ashlynn. She already proved onstage she would humiliate me. I didn't want her to have the chance to humiliate me anymore. Especially while I was wearing her hand-me-downs!

We inched closer to the front of the line.

"Drool," Sam said. "I'm going to ask her out."

"You're going to ask her out?" Sydney, Cashmere, and I all said at the same time.

"She would be an excellent girlfriend." Sam nodded. "Don't get too jealous."

Yeh.

Then I noticed Reilly smoothing his hair down. *Every* guy seemed to be drooling over her. I glanced over and saw Nick in the autograph line behind us. I wondered if he was drooling, too.

"I love how she wears her hair like that," Sydney said to Cashmere.

"Totes," Cashmere agreed.

I noticed Sydney trying to fix her hair to look more like Ashlynn's.

Seriously, Ashlynn could do that to people. She had like superpowers or something.

At camp I wasn't the only one under Ashlynn's spell. Okay, I was the only person who was a slave for her clothes publicly. But everyone else did what she wanted too.

So really, I wasn't surprised Ashlynn was an almost-Broadway star now.

There were about four people ahead of me. It was time to plan my escape.

Achoo! Wachoo!

I fake-sneezed loudly.

"Ew! Disgusting! " Sydney shrieked loudly. What a drama queen.

I hated to be called disgusting, but between Sydney's shriek and my sneeze, Burkle looked over. Good, now I had my escape.

"Go ahead!" I doubled over in a hard-core sneeze position and waved them on. "I don't want to get the star sick. *Achoo!*"

I walked away, toward the back of the line. I stood off to the side, doing a dramatic sneeze now and then when someone looked over at me. I watched as Cashmere quickly got Ashlynn's autograph. Sydney took a long time to get one, since she was probably trying to become BFF with Ashlynn. I watched Ashlynn look freaked as Sam apparently really did ask her out. Sam shrugged and walked away after two seconds.

"Achoo!" I sneezed again.

And then I watched Nick go up and get her autograph. He was there for more than two seconds. He was saying something to Ashlynn. She laughed. She smiled at him. She leaned forward and touched his wrist as he took the autographed picture.

Ugh! She was flirting with Nick, using her Ashlynn Flirting Secret Move! She told us about that secret move at camp!

"I lean forward," she said. "I smile into their eyes. And then I touch their wrist. Gets 'em every time."

"If I looked like you it would," one of the other girls had whined.

"That helps too." Ashlynn had laughed.

Was it working on Nick? Was it working on Nick? Ashlynn was still talking to him, even though there were other people in line. He was smiling. I slumped against the wall.

Me + Ferris wheel fiasco vs. Ashlynn and her Flirting Secret Move? Obviously Ashlynn for the win.

It stunk that when I liked a boy, I couldn't even talk to him! I always made fun of Emma for turning purple when she talked to guys. But Ox liked her! I was destined to be alone for life!!!

(Okay. Sydney wasn't the only drama queen. I'm in seventh grade. I don't need a boyfriend. But . . . it would be nice if I didn't totally screw up any boy *friend*, right? Right. Thank you very much.)

I watched as Ashlynn signed the last picture. Then I saw her looking around.

I shrank against the wall. She couldn't be looking for me, could she? I flattened myself even more. I watched as Mrs. Burkle went over to talk to her.

Whew. She was probably saying thank you, and that it was time for us to leave. And we would see Ashlynn onstage, from the audience. And then?

Never, ever again!

"Attention all Drama Geckos!" Mrs. Burkle called out. I waited for her to announce that we would be leaving. Buh-bye, Ashlynn! See you never!

"Ashlynn has exciting news!" Burkle continued. "She wants to give a few of our students a chance to experience her world as a professional actress! Ashlynn will randomly select one or two of our students to shadow her!"

Everyone was like, Oooh! I hope she picks me! Besides me, of course.

"I'll close my eyes and point to someone," Ashlynn said. She put her hand over her eyes and waved her hand around.

Lucky for me, Tess was tall. Great to hide behind. Sydney was practically knocking people over to get to the front row. Anywhere Ashlynn's pointing went, so did Sydney.

"You!" Ashlynn pointed. At Tess!

I gave her a nudge forward. And that's when Ashlynn kept going.

"The girl in the black shirt with the sparklies!" Ashlynn said.

Tess wasn't wearing a black shirt. She was wearing yellow. And there were no sparklies.

Oh no.

"Payton, she means you!" Tess squealed.

"She couldn't mean me!" I protested, hiding behind her even more. "I was behind you! There was no way!'

"The lucky Dramatic Gecko is . . . hm . . ." Mrs. Burkle was looking, but luckily couldn't see me behind Tess.

"Sydney!" I said. "You go ahead! I don't want it!"

Sydney smiled and started forward.

"Not you," Ashlynn said. "I said black shirt with sparklies. Hiding behind the tall girl."

"Ah, you have selected Payton!" Burkle said.

"Bacon! Come on up!" Ashlynn said.

Everyone cracked up. I stayed frozen behind Tess.

"Actually, it's Paaaaytttton," Mrs. Burkle said, enunciating. "Payton! We're waiting!"

Everyone turned to look at me. There was no way to get out of this. I trudged up to the steps and walked onto the stage.

Ashlynn smiled at me kindly, showing no sign of recognition. I knew this could not be good.

Fourteen

MATHLETICS AUDITORIUM

Finally!!!! We were at the mathletes arena!

Well, actually, we were seated in a school auditorium. But it was exciting, because we were all mathletes.

Three competing schools. Our school was in the middle row—Mrs. James's group on the left side and Coach Babbitt's on the right. Ox was seven seats to my right. I really wanted to try to work things out with Ox, but he was too far away.

So I would have to concentrate 100 percent on the math. I put on my concentration face.

"Thinking about how you stole your sister's boyfriend?" Jazmine whispered to me.

Well, that explained why Jazmine forced her way through everyone to sit next to me. She wanted to distract me.

"I'm thinking about continuing my reign as mathletes champion," I whispered back.

Two could play at that game. Ha.

A woman walked onstage, stood at the podium, and spoke into the microphone:

"Welcome to our school and our mathletic competition! I'm Dana Lindsley, Head coach of the home team."

"Go, Gargoyles!" someone shouted from the front. *Gargoyles? That's even weirder than Geckos.* The home team started chanting loudly: "Go, Gargoyles! Go, Gargoyles! Go, Gargoyles!"

"We are all looking forward to team spirit, good sportsmanship, and most especially . . . fun with math!"

Most of the audience cheered. Jazminc just sat looking bored. I clapped.

A man took the stage and introduced himself as the coach of the visiting team from Brooklyn.

"Go, Panthers!" He said into the microphone, pumping his fist in the air.

"Go! Panthers! Go! Panthers!" His team stood up, shouted, and pumped their fists.

Then Coach Babbitt walked out and took the Panthers' coach's place. The place went quiet.

"I'm Coach Babbitt of—" *Screeeee!* The microphone screeched.

"Ow!"

"Youch!"

Everybody plugged their ears and groaned.

"Sorry," Coach said. "Feedback. As I was saying, I'm Coach Babbitt of the Geckos." *Scree!* He paused, adjusting the microphone.

"Go, Geckos!" Nima shouted. She was sitting next to me, and I jumped a little, not expecting that loud volume coming from her.

"Go, Geckos!" someone down our row yelled. We all started cheering, but our timing was off. It sounded like "Go-Geck-Go-Go-Geck!"

"Okay, it's fixed," Coach Babbitt announced. Our team "cheer" stopped. "I will now read the rules and regulations from the official *Mathletics Handbook*. Rule one point on: All participants must be in the seventh or eighth grade," Coach Babbitt began.

"Daddy!" a small voice called out. "Look at me!"

I froze. I knew that small voice. Everyone's head

turned to look toward the back of the auditorium. And there was Mason Case-Babbitt.

"Watch this!" Mason yelled. *Oh. No. Way.*

Mason was balancing on the back of a seat! He hopped to the seat in the row ahead of him. Hop! Hop! Mason was jumping across the tops of the seats and headed down toward the mathletes.

"Mason!" Coach Babbitt's voice boomed. "Get down before you get—"

"Whoa!" Mason lost his balance and disappeared in between rows. The room was still quiet, until Mason started to wail.

"Ow!!!" he shrieked. "Mommy!"

And there was Counselor Case racing down the aisle. She zoomed into the row where Mason was and picked him up. Mason quieted down.

"He's okay," Counselor case called up to her husband. "Sorry. We just arrived in the city, and Mason's a little overexcited. He'll behave. Please, continue."

Some people from the other schools started giggling. Not the Geckos. We knew from experience how much trouble Mason could be.

"So," Coach Babbitt said, his voice a little shakier than

usual. "The competition consists of two rounds. First, the workbook round, where you will each fill out and answer ten questions to the best of your ability. There will be a break, while the judges score them, and then the team with the highest total score will be announced. Then, the individuals with the top twenty highest scores will compete onstage in the head-to-head lightning round."

"You forgot the calculator rule!" another small, familiar voice yelled. And there, walking across the stage, was Mason's twin brother, Jason. He reached up and took the microphone from his stunned father.

"Rule number two," Jason began.

"He said 'number two'!" Mason shouted from his mother's lap in the back row.

Now everyone was swiveling their heads from the stage to the back row. Jason to Mason back to Jason.

"They're twins!" a girl from another school exclaimed, and the room broke out in giggles.

"Excuse me," Jason said. "This is serious. Rule number two states that calculators *are* allowed in the workbook round, but they are forbidden during the lightning round."

"I have my very own scientific calculator, see?" he said, holding it up.

What was that?

Out of the corner of my eye, I saw a small figure racing by, down the aisle. Mason! I schlumped down. At least this time I was not their tutor. I was not in charge of them. Mason and Jason had nothing to do with me.

"Hey, Emma!" Jason yelled into the microphone. "Hi! I know you're going to beat everyone here tomorrow!"

By now Coach Babbitt had come out of his stupor and was trying to wrest the microphone out of Jason's hands. Mason raced up onto the stage.

"I see Emma too!" he yelled, jumping up and down. Then he bent over and stood on his head.

Everyone in the audience was cracking up. Except me, of course. I schlumped farther and chewed my hair.

"This is a fiasco," I muttered.

"This is hilarious," Jazmine said. "More boy toys for Emma. You'll never be able to focus now."

"Be quiet, Jazmine," I said. I was fed up with Jazmine James and embarrassed by the twins I tutor and annoyed that my big New York City trip was being ruined.

"We're supposed to be on the same team," I hissed at Jazmine.

"There is no 'Jazmine' in 'team,'" Jasmine said. "I

❀ 131 ❀

plan to take number one in individuals, and that's all that matters."

Wow. I intended to get first place myself, but I was also rooting for the Geckos. Jazmine James had been my nemesis since the day I'd met her. She was mean and self-ish then, and obviously nothing had changed.

I looked at the stage and sighed. Coach Babbitt and Counselor Case had corralled the boys and were carrying them off the stage. Things hadn't changed there, either. Mason and Jason were still the terror twins.

I closed my eyes to block out everyone—Jazmine, the twin boys, even Ox. Nothing on this trip was going as planned.

I hoped Payton was having fun right now, because everything here seemed to be one big mess.

Payton

Fifteen

BACK AT THE THEATER

"Ashlynn, what a wonderful thing you are doing," Mrs. Burkle said as we stood in a room off the stage where the set pieces and costumes were stored. "Giving a Drama Gecko a backstage look at being a star."

The rest of the Drama Geckos were in the theater. I could hear them being sent back to their chaperones and groups. I had a sudden longing to be back with Sydney, Jazmine, and even Mrs. James again. Even that would be better than this.

"If someone else wants to do it, they can," I said. "I, um . . . might be catching a cold. *Achoo!*"

I fake-sneezed.

"I don't want to get the star of the show sick," I said, sniffling. "I better go back to the hotel with everyone else."

"Although you do look kind of sick, it's probably just nerves," Ashlynn said. "I'm sure you're not used to being around a celebrity."

"Nothing to be nervous about," Mrs. Burkle said. "We already see what a friendly, generous person Ashlynn is."

Ashlynn flashed me a (fake) smile.

"But I don't know who my roommates are!" I said. "I won't know where to go!"

"I'll send one of our parent chaperones to pick you up," Mrs. Burkle said to me. "Enjoy, you two!"

"Wait! You're leaving me alone with her?" I said, panicky. I needed witnesses! Ashlynn was totally going to torture me. I just knew it.

"I have an adult guardian with me at all times," Ashlynn said. "Because of my age. So you're fine."

"Wonderful," Burkle said.

"But—" I said.

"No buts!" Burkle said. "Payton, I shall leave you now. Make us Geckos proud! I can only imagine what a fabulous time you two will have here in the heart of the theater!"

I could only imagine Tessa and Reilly and Sam and Nick . . . sigh. Everyone was all, Yay! Let's go see the hotel! Let's go see our rooms!

Except me! Because I was stuck here! With Ashlynn, and Jane, who came up to us.

"I just adore your shirt." Ashlynn smiled at me. "TC Couture, isn't it?"

"It *is* an adorable shirt," Jane said innocently. "It seems like something Ashlynn would wear. You two have the same taste in clothes."

"I know, right?" Ashlynn said. "I so totally would have worn that shirt . . . last year."

The insult went right over Jane's head.

"Ah, memories. I'm remembering when Bertha Burkle and I first met as two young thespians," Jane said. "Oh, the glory of friendships formed over the theater. You two chitchat and get to know each other."

She left us alone.

I took a deep breath and waited for it.

"Payton," Ashlynn said. "Payton, Payton, Payton. What a surprise."

"For me, too," I said.

"I was surprised you didn't tell all your friends that you knew me," Ashlynn said. "You would have gained popularity points for sure. Between knowing me and your shirt, you could be the coolest Dramatic Gecko today."

"I wasn't sure you recognized me," I said. That, and I knew she had such great potential to humiliate me, which was proven true anyway.

"I didn't," Ashlynn said. "You're so much paler now. But I definitely recognized my shirt and was like, Hey! That's my old shirt that I gave to . . ."

Don't say it don't say it . . .

"Summer Slave!" Ashlynn laughed.

She said it.

"Isn't this the most amazing coincidence?" Ashlynn said. "My Summer Slave is here. And about to be my Stage Slave!"

Her what? *Stage Slave?* Nooo! Not in NYC! I'd already done my time under the stage for community service. I'd done my time!

I had to say no. I thought about what Emma used to say to me at camp.

"Just stand up for yourself," Emma said. "Just say no to her. She's manipulating you."

"But this is the only way I can get the coolest clothes for middle school," I had said to Emma. "I just have to do it for a couple weeks. Then I'll never have to do it again. I'll never see this girl again."

Augh! I didn't know I'd see her again.

"Hm, you could clean my dressing room!" Ashlynn said, tapping her finger on her chin. "It's totally trashed."

"I'm not cleaning your dressing room," I said firmly.

"We don't have a latrine here," Ashlynn said. "Remember latrine duty, and we were all like, What does that mean? Ew! Cleaning the bathroom? Gross. So I got you to do it, remember?"

How could I forget? I traded for a tank top and jeans. Oh, crud, the jeans I was wearing right now. Ashlynn and I both looked down at the same moment.

"Hey, you're wearing my jeans too!" Ashlynn said. "Wow, I knew you were a Fashlynn wannabe but, whoa. How embarrassing. Don't you even have any clothes of your own?"

Yes. Yes, I did. But I wanted to wear my coolest clothes, the ones that would fit in NYC best. Which of course were Ashlynn's shirt, jeans, and . . .

Oh no, I realized, this would only get worse. The dress I had brought to wear to the show tonight? Also Ashlynn's.

At least when I was Summer Slave I'd gotten clothes for it. But as Stage Slave I would get nothing.

I needed to do it. I needed stand up for myself, once and for all. I closed my eyes so I couldn't see her smirking at me. I took a deep breath.

"Ashlynn," I said.

"Ashlynn!" a voice also said at the same time. Louder and more forceful than mine, that's for sure.

I opened my eyes. I had a quick glimpse of a woman in black sticking her head in the door. But that's all I saw of her because my attention went elsewhere fast.

"They are driving me up a wall," the woman said. "The dog walker didn't show again. Here they are."

"They" were three little poofballs that she popped through the door. One. Two. Three!

Three little fluffy dogs! All of them were little, white fluffballs.

"Oh, how cute," I said.

And oh, how . . . spazzy! They were yapping and running right at me. And then three poofballs were jumping all over my legs.

"Mother!" Ashlynn yelled.

"I'll be back after my nail appointment," the woman said. "Ta-ta."

"Um, down, girls!" I said. "Or boys."

They were jumping all over and licking my jeans. And my sneakers. And . . . I saw a little orange dust on one of the dogs.

Oh yeah—the cheese-puff explosion! The dogs were going crazy licking the cheese puff crumbs from my clothes.

And not just licking, chewing. And ouch—biting.

"A little help here?" I said. "Ashlynn? Random dogs are attacking me?"

"They're not random," Ashlynn said, calmly applying lip gloss. "They're mine."

I leaned down to pull one off my shoe. And another one jumped up and latched on to my hair.

"Your dog is attached to my head!" I said. "Can you please call your dogs off?"

"Down, Bebe," Ashlynn said in a bored voice. "Down, Barbra. Down, LeaMichele."

The dogs jumped even crazier. Yeesh. They didn't listen to her and they didn't even acknowledge her. But they were all over me. And they were really cute, even though seriously insane.

Then one of the dogs rolled onto her back and panted at me.

"Oh, cute," I said. "I'll scritch your belly if you don't eat my head."

I started scritching her belly. Then the other two dropped in front of me also.

Suddenly I was scritching three dog bellies.

"They're totally annoying," Ashlynn said. "I got them because I saw this Mera Padley bag? And I found out it was a dog carrier. So I got some dogs. But they won't all fit in the bag, so it was useless."

"Ashlynn, they're so cute," I said. "Come here. Scratch a belly."

"Uk, no," Ashlynn said. "They're getting fur all over your—my—TC Couture T-shirt."

Her cell phone rang.

"Yes." Ashlynn rolled her eyes. "Fine. I said, Fine."

Ashlynn hung up and turned to me.

"Time for your grand tour," Ashlynn said.

"Oh!" I said. Cool! A tour! Maybe she was just kidding about me being her Stage Slave, after all. Or at least, whoever was on the phone told her to be nice to me?

Whatever. I'd take it.

"Follow me," Ashlynn said.

Ooh, where were we going? A rehearsal area? The dressing rooms? The costume room?

I stood up and tried to brush fur/cheese puff dust off of me. The dogs started running around in circles, yapping again.

"Can you grab the leashes?" Ashlynn said, and didn't wait for an answer.

Okay, that was more of a challenge than it sounded as I had to chase the dogs around in their circles and try to grab their trailing leashes. Finally I had all three.

"Ready!" I told Ashlynn, slightly out of breath.

Ashlynn waved for me to follow her.

"This way, Bebe! Or is that Barbra?" I said. I held out the leash to Ashlynn.

"Do you mind holding their leashes?" Ashlynn asked me.

"All three?" I looked down at the dogs tangling up in their leashes as they started jumping at my jeans again.

The dogs started yipping louder. They were excited to go where we were going. So was I!

Ashlynn pushed through a door and we were—

Outside in a teeny courtyard in the back of the building. The dogs dragged me over to a small patch of grass and started sniffing. Barbra—or was it LeaMichele—squatted down and—

"You'll need this," Ashlynn said, tossing me a small box.

What?

"Poop bags," Ashlynn said. "Get to work, Stage Slave."

And she went back inside the building, leaving me with three squatting dogs.

Sixteen

THE HOTEL

"Pomeranian poo." Payton finished telling me about what happened to her after the mathletes had left the theater.

"Ew!" I grimaced. "Gross! TMY!" I said.

"It's TM*I*," my twin sister grumbled. "And so far *that* has been the highlight of my first day in New York City."

"Hey, twins!" Cashmere's head popped out of a doorway. "We're right next door to you! Sydney, we can bang on the wall and the twins will hear it."

"Whatever," Sydney's voice said from their room.

Payton and I were carrying our suitcases and bags through the hotel hallway to our room.

"Room 817," I announced. Cool. A prime number.

"We're here?" Payton gasped. "Emma, we are about to enter . . . drumroll, please . . . our very own hotel room in New York City!"

I slid the room key card the way the hotel front desk person had shown us.

The little light on the door flickered red.

"Isn't it supposed to be green?" my twin asked.

I slid the card again. Red blinking light. I flipped the card around. Swipe. Nothing.

"Having trouble, twins?" Jazmine James walked by. "You want to win mathletes, but you can't even get into your room?" She cackled.

I waited for Hector's echoing cackle. Nothing. Then I remembered the eighth floor was all girls. The boys were on the ninth. For once I didn't have to deal with Jazmine's sidekick.

Although one of the eighth-grade mathletes was with her.

"Hi, Emily," the girl said, looking at both Payton and me.

"Hi." I smiled weakly. Swipe. Red. Flip. Red. Rotate. Red light again.

Jazmine and the girl, who was apparently her roommate, went up to the door just past ours. Jazmine swooped her key card, and the two girls disappeared into their room.

"This card must be defective," I complained, jiggling it.

"Oh, give it to me," my twin sister said, "*Emily*."

I handed over the card.

"Like you can do it better than me, *Pain-ton*," I scoffed. "You couldn't even open the right locker on the first day . . ."

"We're in!" Payton squealed.

The door opened on her first try.

"Woo," my twin said, "hoo?"

Our hotel room was more like a hotel closet, really. It had enough room for two twin-sized (appropriate) beds and a shallow closet. And a stall-sized bathroom.

"What?" I said. "You were expecting them to put a bunch of middle-schoolers in a luxury suite?"

"It's cozy," Payton determined, "and all ours." She wheeled her travel suitcase in. I followed with mine. I placed my backpack on a bed.

"Ooh." My sister smiled. "You gave me the bed with a window view!"

"It's probably a view of a wall," I said, opening my

backpack. *Aah . . . my mathlete review books.* "Or one of those giant billboards advertising mattresses."

"Or it could be a View! Of! New! York! City!" Payton said, pulling the cord to open the curtains.

"Oh!" she said. I walked over next to her and looked out the window.

"Wow," I breathed. We were overlooking the building next door's rooftop garden. Plants and flowers flourishing right in the center of the city.

"Look down," Payton whispered.

From our height we could clearly see all the people walking on the sidewalks, heading into restaurants, hailing taxis.

Payton and I looked at each other and grinned.

"New York City!" we shouted at the exact same time.

Bang! Bang! There was knocking on one side of the room.

"Shush up, twins!" Sydney's voice came through the wall.

"Yeah! Keep it down! Some people are trying to study!" Jazmine's voice came through the opposite wall.

"We are surrounded . . . ," Payton said.

"By evil!" I finished. "But will our evil nemeses bring us down? I say no! Twin powers activate!"

Payton giggled, but then her face changed.

"We don't need them to bring us down." She sighed, sitting on her bed. "I'm already down."

"Because of Ashlynn." I shook my head. "You really need to learn to stick up for yourself better. You can't let the Ashlynns of the world walk all over you."

"It's not just Ashlynn," my twin said. Then she told me about how halfway through the Ferris wheel ride, she'd gotten dizzy and nauseous.

"I think Nick thought I wasn't happy to be with him," she finished.

Uh-oh.

"Um," I said, "actually, Nick wasn't in the best mood after we left the toy store. He said something like he'd misunderstood a situation."

"I knew it! Augh!" Payton flopped facedown on the bed and pulled a pillow over her head.

"Your reaction is leading me to one conclusion," I said. "You like Nick."

"Drrf," Payton said from under the pillow.

"What?"

"Yrrf erf lerrf Nrf," she said, muffled.

I leaned over my bed, which was about two inches away from my sister's, and yanked the pillow off.

 147

"What?" I repeated.

Payton sat up. Her face was red.

"Duh," she said. "I said, 'Duh, yes I like Nick.'"

"Oooh!" I remembered how Payton had acted when she first found out I had a crush on Ox. "Payton and Nick, up in a tree, k-i-s-s—"

"Shhh!" Suddenly *my* face was covered with a pillow. My twin sister was trying to smother me!

"Sydney and Jazmine will hear us!" she hissed, removing the pillow. Okay, Payton wouldn't really try to smother me. But still.

I shook my hair out of my face and regained my composure.

"Well, good luck with the whole Nick thing," I said, and sat back on my pillow. I opened *Mathletes Review* book 17, kicked off my sneakers, and settled in to study.

"*Helloo . . .*," Payton said. "Traumatized twin over here."

"Payton." I sighed. "Do you really want boy advice from *me*?" Boys completely baffled me. I needed to focus on problems I *could* solve.

Like combinatorics. *What is the greatest integer . . .*

"Let's review," I said. "You like Nick and Nick likes you, but he thinks you don't. I like Ox, but everyone thinks I like Nick. Which I don't. I mean, not how I like Ox."

I took a breath and kept my voice low so only my sister, and not the neighboring rooms—villainesses—could hear.

"I have absolutely no clue what to do about B-O-Y-S, but I can't think about it now, because I am an elite mathlete in training."

I continued reading: *What is the greatest integer between 1,000 and 1,250 that can be divided evenly by—*

Knock! Knock!

"Yoohoo!" Mrs. Burkle's voice boomed through the door. "Everybody change into your bathing suits! It's time to go to the swimming pool!"

Payton popped up off the bed.

"Swimming poooool!" She squealed and grabbed her suitcase and ran into the bathroom.

I could hear more squeals coming from the direction of Sydney and Cashmere's room.

Ugh. I needed earplugs to drown out the distractions.

"Emma!" Payton called. "Are you getting ready out there?"

"No," I said. "I am sitting out here. With my books. I am studying, not swimming."

Knock! Knock!

"Girls!" Mrs. Burkle called. "You have two more minutes to get ready. And remember, this activity is not optional. All Geckos to the pool!"

What?

Now I heard complaining through the wall from Jazmine's side.

"No exceptions!" trilled Mrs. Burkle.

Drat. Drat to the infinitieth power. I opened my suitcase and took out the swimsuit my mother had forced me to pack. And then, in a smaller pocket next to my clothes, I saw them.

Yes! My flash cards! I had almost forgotten the color-coded review cards I'd made especially for elite competitions.

Okay, then. I would get into a swimsuit and flip-flops and go down to the pool with the rest of the people. And then I'd find a nice spot out of the way to study.

A mathlete always finds a way to do math.

Payton came out of the bathroom in her signature pink suit with a towel wrapped around her waist.

"My turn!" I said cheerfully as we maneuvered around each other in the small space. My twin eyed me suspiciously as I held up my turquoise suit with one hand and backed into the bathroom.

I shut the door. In my other hand were my math flashcards.

Ha. Payton hadn't noticed. I'd make sure to keep them hidden in my towel until we got to the pool. Plan saved!

Seventeen

AT THE HOTEL POOL

"No running! No diving!"

Mrs. James was standing at the door that led to the pool. A group of us were all bunched up around her, wearing bathing suits and wrapped in towels.

"Okay!" we all shouted, and started to move to the door.

"No spitting!" Mrs. James shouted, putting her arms up to block the door. "No floating facedown and pretending you're dead and sending the chaperones into a panic."

"Okay!" we all said.

She opened the door and a blast of chlorine smell

hit me in the face. Yeah! We all went into the pool area and took over. We had the whole place to ourselves. (Well, as soon as the lady who was in the pool saw us coming and fled.)

There was a mad rush for the chairs sitting around the pool. I threw my towel on a chair right next to the deep end and Tess grabbed the chair next to mine.

I noticed Emma going to the area farthest from the pool. With her flash cards.

"Ready?" Tess asked me.

We went to the side of the pool. I dipped my toe in the water. Brrr. I decided to sit on the edge and go in gently.

"Cannonball!" someone yelled. And Sam went flying right past me and did a cannonball. And soaked us.

"Eeee!" Tess and I shrieked. Then we looked at each other.

"Cannonball!" we yelled. And Tess and I cannonballed in too.

"No doing that, either!" Mrs. James shouted.

"Oh, pish," Mrs. Nicely called to her from across the pool. "Relax and let the kids have some fun."

Yeah! That was the goal here, to relax and have some fun. Pretty much everyone was in the pool. Sydney and

Cashmere were in the shallow end, not getting their hair wet. Except Emma. I looked around but didn't see Ox. Or Nick.

Well, their loss. I dived under the water and did a somersault. I attempted a handstand, but I tipped over. Then I sank to the bottom and sat there. I couldn't see much of anything but the hair floating around my face.

Ah. It was relaxing. It was nice to just float. Floating my cares away . . . I floated next to the wall.

And then a foot stuck in front of my face.

I popped up out of the water.

"Excuse me!" The girl from Emma's mathletes team, Nima, was sitting on the edge of the pool. "May I bother you for a minute? In private?"

I looked over at Tess, who shrugged at me.

"Okay," I said, and pulled myself onto the edge and out of the pool. "Let me get a towel."

I grabbed one of the scratchy hotel towels and wrapped it around me.

"It's urgent," Nima said urgently as she half dragged me across the pool area.

What? Was it something about Emma? Oh no, was something wrong with Emma? I looked over at Emma, who was sitting at a little table with her math flashcards out. She was muttering to herself.

Oh no, did Nima think Emma had gone *crazy*? That her obsessive mathness had put her *over the edge*? I followed Nima out of the pool area and into the hallway. She looked at me with panic in her eyes and took a deep breath.

"It's insanity." Nima said, confirming my suspicions right away.

"Oh no," I said. "You think it's really that bad?"

"Worse," Nima said. "Nonstop thinking about math and numbers and equations all day, and then in nightmares at night. Obsessing over the math trophy and stressing about what happens if the Mathletic Geckos lose in New York City? And thinking, Then what would be the point of coming down here?!"

Whoa. I needed to call my parents if Emma was really this wigged-out. I got goose bumps, and not just from the air-conditioning that was blasting in the freezing hallway.

"Thanks for sharing, Nima," I said to her. "I'm glad you thought you could trust me."

"Oh, I don't trust you," she said to me. "I just thought you'd know how I felt and I had to spill to somebody.

But you're still competition, so that means you're my nemesis, Emma."

Emma?

Emma?

Oh my gosh. Nima thought I was Emma. She'd mixed us up!

"Nima!" I said. "First of all, I think you need to talk to Coach Babbitt. Or your parents or something. You're way too stressed. Second of all, I'm not Emma. I'm Payton."

"Payton?" Nima looked slightly horrified. "You're Payton?"

I nodded. I guess with my wet hair in a ponytail and wearing a bathing suit for the pool it would be even harder to tell us apart. Speaking of wet hair, mine was starting to get seriously cold out here in the air-conditioned hall. I wrapped my towel tighter to stop me from shivering.

"You're not even on mathletes," Nima said. "Why am I telling you this?"

"Um," I said. "A mix-up. But I can still help you."

"I've wasted four whole minutes of time that I could have spent studying! Oh no!" Nima said.

I wasn't sure what to answer. I just shivered in my wet bathing suit and towel. I made a mental note to tell Coach Babbitt about Nima's stress.

"Payton?" Someone was coming down the hall. At least someone could tell who I was. I turned around to see Tess.

"Hi, Nima," she said. "Mrs. James says she wants everyone in the pool area so she can supervise."

"No problem," Nima said. "I need to go study."

She walked off, leaving me alone with Tess in the hallway.

"Hi-i-i," I said, my teeth chattering a little. From cold. I followed Tess back down the hall toward the pool.

"Isn't swimming so much fun?" Tess asked, looking through the window at everyone in the pool. "Too bad Nick had to miss it."

"Yeh," I said. "I wonder where he is."

"What?" Tess said. "You don't know? Didn't you get his text?"

What text? "Um, no."

"You're not the only one who's getting a cool break on this trip," Tess said. "Nick got to go on a tour with Ashlynn this evening!"

What?

"Yeah, Ashlynn chose him to go on a tour next," Tess said. "Ashlynn is going to show him their professional lightboard and sound system. How cool is that? It's like Nick's dream come true."

I shivered.

"Hey, you're freezing," Tess said. "Let's go back into the pool. Aren't heated pools awesome?"

Awesome! Yeah! I had to forget about Nick while he had his fun with Ashlynn! Ashlynn could make all his dreams come true!

I stood shivering for a second. Grrr. Then I pushed my way into the pool area. I felt the warmth of the humidity blast over me. Then I felt the heat of my frustration blast over me.

I marched over to Emma. I couldn't do anything about Nick falling in love with Ashlynn. Ashlynn was irresistible. Fine. But I could do something about Emma.

"Emma," I said. "You are not going to Nima out."

"What are you talking about?" Emma said.

I took Emma's flash cards. I marched over to the pool. And I tossed them in.

"Hey!" Emma yelled. "What the—"

"You know those by heart," I said. "Staring at them and muttering is so not going to help you. But this will. Some fun."

I reached over. And I pushed.

Splash!

Emma into the pool.

"Are you crazy?" Emma resurfaced, soaking wet and floating among her flashcards.

"No and neither are you," I said.

"Twin fight!" someone yelled.

"Not a twin fight," I yelled back. "We're on the same team! It's twins against the world!"

I went over to a bin and pulled out some beach balls. I tossed one to Emma Then I punched one at Sam, hitting him on the head.

"Score!" I yelled. I threw a bunch of beach balls into the pool.

Everyone started laughing and jumping for the balls. Then they were hitting balls to one another. Everyone was having fun. Except Emma, who was collecting her soggy flash cards. I grabbed them up quickly and put them on the side of the pool.

And then the pool door opened. Everyone stopped and looked. A bunch of other kids we didn't know came into the pool area.

"It's the Panthers team," Emma said, narrowing her eyes. "They're seeded number three in the competition."

"Geckos versus Panthers!" I yelled. And I threw a beach ball toward the Brooklyn team.

One of the girls caught it.

 159

I looked at Emma.

"It's a competition," I said. Emma grinned.

"Go Geckos!" Emma yelled. "Crush the Panthers!"

Then the Panthers all jumped in the pool too. And before I knew it, the Geckos were on one side of the pool. The Panthers (most of them, anyway) were on the other side.

And we were punching balls back and forth.

"You're getting my hair wet!" Sydney protested.

Emma responded by bopping a ball over at Sydney and Cashmere, getting close enough to splash them.

"Eeee!" They both squealed. And moved away from us.

Good, I thought. *Stay away if you're not gonna play.*

"Two four six eight, Geckos Geckos are really great!" Emma shouted.

"Two, four, sixteen squared! Panthers team is more prepared!" a Panther yelled back.

Emma responded by nailing the Panther in the head with a beach ball.

"Nice shot," I told her admiringly.

Emma grinned at me. And we both tossed beach balls to the other side of the pool.

Emma

Eighteen

THE HOTEL POOL

"Hi-ya!" I punched a beach ball at the other team and lost my footing. Before I slipped under the water, I saw it bounce off a boy Panther's head. *Bull's-eye!*

I held my breath underwater and regained my balance. I popped up through the surface, ready for my next victim. But something was weird. All of the sound around me was muffled, like someone had turned the volume down to low. Very low.

"Payton!" I called. I located my twin and paddled over to her. "Payton."

". . . ," Payton said, looking at me.

"I can't hear you!" I told her. "I can't hear anything! My ears are plugged up!"

"..." Payton frowned. Her lips kept moving.

"I'm going up to the room!" I said.

My twin finally got it. She nodded and pointed up. She also pointed to Mrs. Nicely.

"I'll tell the chaperone," I agreed. I got out of the pool, wrapped a towel around me, and tried to dry off my hair and the insides of my ears.

Nothing. The whole pool area must have been noisy, but I couldn't hear it. I went over to Mrs. Nicely and explained my situation. She gave me my room key card and pointed up. Then she said something to a lifeguard, and together we left the pool area.

Squinch, squinch. My ears made sloshing sounds as Mrs. Nicely and I silently walked through the corridor on the way to the elevator.

We reached the lobby elevators and stepped into an open one. While waiting for the doors to close, I spotted Nick coming in the hotel entrance.

"!" His mouth was moving. He held up a mini-camera and waved it around.

The elevator doors shut. I had no idea what Nick was trying to tell me. The elevator went up to my floor.

✿ 162 ✿

The doors opened. Mrs. Nicely and I walked down to my room.

Squirch! There was a weird, echoing sound in my left ear. I tilted my head and jumped on my left foot, a trick my mother had taught me. A useless trick. *Wee-oo-wee-ooh* went my right ear.

I felt a little dizzy. As I slid my room card in the swiper, I tilted over.

A couple of eighth graders—Katelyn and Ava, I remembered—were walking down the hallway in my direction. They saw me hopping and swaying and started giggling. I couldn't hear them, but I could definitely tell they were laughing at me.

"I have vestibular issues, okay?" I yelled, just before I lost my balance and fell over.

I lay sprawled at Mrs. Nicely's feet. I looked up and noticed the red light blinking. I hadn't gotten my door open either. Double humiliation.

My library media specialist/chaperone pulled me up and got my card to work. I assured her I was fine and said good-bye as she left to go back down to the pool.

I didn't know if she'd said anything to me. But at least she was gone. I looked around my little room. Alone at last. Perfect time to study.

I remembered my floating flash cards as I changed into a new white with blue stripes shorts and tee set. The flash cards were a total loss, I thought as I combed my wet hair in the bathroom. But my outfit was cute, I decided as I looked in the mirror.

My mother had taken Payton and me shopping for this trip. My twin and I had picked out one casual outfit. Our mother . . . well, she'd insisted on buying us matching dresses. They were hideous.

"No, Mom!" Payton and I had protested.

"You may need them for a dressy occasion," she had said firmly. "Besides, they're sixty percent off!"

Yeah, because no one would buy them.

I finished drying off, thinking about the matching dresses tucked into the bottom of our suitcases. Which is where they would stay.

Unlike my math books, which were out, all ready to be reread for the fiftieth time. I looked at the clock. Four thirty. Plenty of time to study before our next activity—dinner at six thirty. Yes!

Squoish, my right ear gurgled. This was seriously annoying. I would have to ignore the water sloshing in my eustachian tubes in order to study for tomorrow's competition.

Tomorrow's competition!

"Aaaaaaah!" I yelled. (It sounded like "aaaaaaah" to me.)

The competition! What if I couldn't hear by then? What if my ears stayed clogged? I would be disqualified from competing! Sure, I could do the written part, but the lightning round was all oral. If I couldn't hear the questioner, I couldn't answer the questions!

I banged the sides of my head desperately. No change. This was a disaster! I flopped down on my bed with a yelp of frustration.

There had to be a way to fix this! Maybe sign language? Okay, I didn't know sign language. What was I going to do???

Zzzzzzz . . . I fell asleep.

Pop! Poppity—pop-pop!

I woke up when the inside of my skull exploded. (Or was that part of my dream?) I opened my eyes and saw Payton looking down at me.

"How are you doing?" she asked.

"Okay." I yawned and looked at the clock. It was 4:50. Nice, little nap . . .

"Hey!" I jumped up. "I heard you! Payton, I can hear!" The popping must have been my ears draining.

"Talk to me, Pay!" I exclaimed. "I want to hear your voice! Wait, I can hear my own voice now, which is identical to your voice. So never mind, you don't need to say anything."

Payton talked anyway. "Emma, did we get any calls? Or texts?"

"Um," I said. "I don't think so."

My twin looked sad for a moment. Then she picked up her cell phone from the side table.

"I've got five new messages!" she said. "And you have four!" she added, picking up mine.

"Oh," I realized. "I was so worried about not being able to hear, I forgot to check."

"Nick!" Payton said, realization dawning. "Tess, Mom, and Nick *again*!"

I scrolled down mine. Mom, Ox, and Nick?

I skipped over my mom and opened Ox's.

Em- did you get Nick's msg? CU soon! Ox

I opened Nick's message.

"It says Nick wants us to meet in the conference room on the first floor," I read.

"I know, I know," my twin said. "I got the same text. And it says it's a *secret* meeting. What the heck is this all about?"

"I don't know." I shrugged. "But we're supposed to be there at five. That's in exactly five minutes."

"Five minutes?" Payton shrieked. She grabbed her suitcase and dragged it into the bathroom with her. I was surprised they both fit.

I used the time to text Ox and Nick that we'd be there. Then I texted my mother back that we were great, everything was great, and that we'd call her later.

That took four minutes.

"I'm ready!" Payton opened the bathroom door. She'd changed into her cute new outfit (cream shirt and pink leggings). "That was the fastest I've ever gotten ready."

"Congratulations on your new world record," I told her. "But your hair is still damp."

"So is yours," Payton pointed out. "And it's sticking out funny in the back."

Erg! Poolhead plus bedhead. I grabbed a hair band and tied my hair back into a ponytail.

"Better," my twin said. "Now let's go find out what this mystery meeting is all about."

We took the elevator to floor one and followed a sign to the conference room.

"If this clandestine meeting gets us in trouble, I'm

going to say you made me come," I told my sister. "We are *supposed* to be resting in our rooms."

"What?" Payton looked at me like, *Are you crazy?*

I can't afford to get disqualified tomorrow," I explained. We reached the conference room. Nick was at the door.

"Come on in," he said quietly.

We stepped into the room.

"Well, if we get caught, you're not the only mathlete going down," Payton murmured.

Wow.

The conference room was large and brightly lit. There was a rectangular table in the center with a huge flower arrangement on it. A sign sticking out from the flowers read, *Welcome, Matsumo Motor Company!*

"The Matsumo Company plane had mechanical trouble, so they were stuck in Tokyo," Nick said. "So we get the room instead."

Nick moved the flowers, and my jaw dropped. Seated around the conference table were—Tess, Ox, Jazmine, and Hector!

"Five of us plus twins equals all of us," Nick announced. "We're all here."

"Wow, you should've been a mathlete," Tess teased.

Payton walked over and sat down next to Tess.

"Seriously," I said. "Should we be in here?"

"It's okay," Nick said. "Quinton—the limo driver who brought me back from the theater—is married to this hotel's assistant manager. He hooked me up with this room because it's for a good cause."

I sat down next to Payton.

"What cause?" I whispered to my twin. "The Ashlynn Fan Club Foundation?"

Payton kicked me under the table. *Ow*.

Ox leaned across the table.

"Hi, Emma," he said. "Sorry I missed you at the pool. I got there late because I was helping Coach Babbitt carry some math stuff up to his room, and Mason and Jason kept punching all the buttons on the elevator."

Ox smiled at me. He didn't seem mad or anything. Yay, me! I smiled back and felt my face turn red.

"Okay," Jazmine said. "Enough chitchat. I need to get back to studying. What is so important that you brought us down here?"

"Yeah," Hector said, echoing his leader. "What?"

"This is what," Nick said. Suddenly the lights dimmed and a big screen came down, covering one wall.

"I've hooked my minicam up to the projector so we can all see this."

"This" was Ashlynn's face, huge on-screen and smiling.

"Told you," I whispered to Payton.

"Hi! I'm Ashlynn, star of the off-Broadway musical *Fairytale Mash-up*! Nick has asked me to tape a little segment for all you Gecko Hick-o's!"

"Did she just call us hicks?" Tess said.

"So here we are in the dressing room that I share with another actress, um . . ."

"Liz," said an older girl. The camera turned toward her for a moment. I recognized her from the play rehearsal.

"So after we finish your—whatch'callit—HOGS cast?"

"VOGS cast," Nick said, correcting her. We could only hear his voice because he was behind the camera.

Pause.

"This is where I set up my tripod stand and put my camera in it, aiming at Ashlynn," off-screen, real-life Nick said. "That's important to know, considering what comes next."

"What comes next?" Tess, Payton, and I all said at the same time.

"And why should we care?" grumbled Jazmine.

"Just watch," Nick told us. Unpause.

"So after you film this, Nicky, do you want to go do something *fun*?" Ashlynn batted her eyelashes. Which looked gigantic on the screen.

"Um, oh, I've got to get back to the hotel," Nick's voice replied.

"Just a little dinner . . . and maybe a stroll or something romantic?" Ashlynn persisted.

"No, thank you," Nick's voice said more firmly. "Now, would you mind telling me how you got your part in this production?"

"Yes, I mind!" Ashlynn's face suddenly turned mean. "And I need to rehearse in private. So get out!"

"Wait, I just need . . ." Nick's voice said.

"I said *out*!" Ashlynn got up, and we all heard a door slam. Pause.

Our conference room was silent as Nick pressed "pause" on the camera again and said, "I just wanted to get my camera. But it stayed in there with her—still filming. And I wasn't sure at that point what I was supposed to do. Leave? I didn't even know how I was getting back to the hotel. So I waited down the hall a ways. After a little while Ashlynn and Liz left the room and went the opposite way from me. So I ran in and grabbed my camera and tripod. Then I went to the front of the theater, where I found Quinton, who was supposed to drive me back here.

"And on the ride home, I watched the footage of what happened after I left," Nick said. "She'd given me permission to film, and I thought I could find *something* to use in the VOGS cast. I found something all right. This."

He pressed a button on the camera.

"Gah, he wasn't that cute anyway." Ashlynn sat back down by Liz. She was half off-camera, but we could hear her loud and clear.

"Can you believe that bunch of Hick-o's today?" Ashlynn snorted. "Their so-called actors were so lame, complete amateurs."

"I'm not sure they were all drama kids," Liz said.

"Oh yeah, the math nerds." Ashlynn rolled her eyes. "They're even worse than, like, band geeks."

"Hey!" Hector spoke up. "I am an elite mathlete *and* an accomplished cellist. Who does she think she is?"

"Oh, who cares?" Jazmine said. "Calm down."

"And that Wicked Witch girl?" Ashlynn laughed. "Worst. Acting. Ever. She had absolutely no stage presence."

"She did *not* just say that," Jazmine said, her voice

turning deadly. "She wants to see me do wicked? I'll give her evil so bad she'll run screaming off the stage, crying for her mommy."

Pause.

We all looked at Jazmine.

"What?" She glared at us. "Can we finish this up?"

"It's almost done," Nick said. "But I want to warn you. It's kind of hard to watch. I had no idea she'd get so mad at me when I turned her down."

"It's not Nick she's mad at," I whispered to Payton. "It's you. *Us*."

"I know," Payton whispered back.

"Dude, don't blame yourself," Ox told Nick. "She asked me out too."

What? Excuse me? ? ?

"I said no, of course," Ox said. He was looking at me! He was looking at me!

I smiled back at him and gave him a thumbs-up. He grinned back. Yes!

Unpause.

"A school of losers," Ashlynn kept babbling. "Especially those twins. Did you see the one wannabe in last month's fashions and the other one in *sweatpants*?" She cracked up.

"They're yoga pants," I protested.

"Shhh . . ." Everyone shushed me.

"Well, they haven't seen anything yet." Ashlynn laughed. "Tomorrow's show is audience participation, and I'm going to embarrass those Gecko Hick-o's even more. I'm talking Total. Public. Humiliation."

There was a background noise, and then three of the floofiest dogs I'd ever seen raced in and started jumping on Ashlynn.

"Get down!" Ashlynn shrieked. "You'll get my skirt all muddy."

And she pushed—*pushed*—one dog off her lap. We couldn't see it hit the floor, but we heard a sad, hurt whimper.

The screen went black.

And we all just sat there.

Payton

Nineteen

STILL IN THE HOTEL CONFERENCE ROOM

Everyone was silent.

"Well, that was exceptionally harsh," Tess said. "What did *we* ever do to her?"

"I know *some* people might think you two boys are attractive," Jazmine said, looking at Ox and Nick, "but is that enough for public humiliation?"

I shifted uncomfortably in my seat.

"Yes, I believe it is!" Emma said suddenly. "Um . . . think of it this way. Say I happened to like either Nick or *Ox*—"

"You like Nick and Ox?!" Hector said. "I knew it! That explains the whole Ferris wheel thing."

Nick and Ox both turned red.

"*No, no!*" Emma shouted. "I was speaking hypo-thetically. I do *not* like Nick and Ox. Well, not Nick. I mean—I'm just saying, for example, if I were Ashlynn and asked out Nick and Ox and they turned me down, I might get a little upset."

"That wasn't *upset*," Hector said. "She's talking total *annihilation* of all of us."

"Well, Ox *is* really special," Emma babbled on. "I mean Nick *and* Ox are . . ."

I knew she was trying to save me. I appreciated it. But I didn't want her to have to go any further.

I knew what I needed to do.

"Emma, it's okay!" I said, cutting her off. I stood up and looked at everyone. "I have a confession to make."

Everyone looked back at me, confused. Except Emma, who gave me a look like, was I sure I wanted to do this?

"The reason Ashlynn hates us is . . ." I took a deep breath. "Me. Ashlynn and I went to summer camp together."

Everyone was like "What?!"

"I should have said something right away," I said. "But I was so shocked. And then I thought she didn't

❀ 176 ❀

recognize me so I thought I could stay under the radar."

"Why is that a big deal?" Jazmine asked. "You could have said hi and gone on with your lives."

I glanced at Emma.

"Let's just say Ashlynn and Payton didn't get along at camp," Emma said. "And leave it at that."

"What the heck did you do to her?" Hector asked.

"Nothing!" Emma and I both said.

"It's what I did *for* her," I said softly.

"Payton, you don't have to say anything else," Emma said. She tilted her head toward Jazmine and Hector. Then at Tess. And . . . Nick.

And I realized that was exactly why I wanted to say what I said next.

"I want to be honest," I said. "I don't want Ashlynn to have anything to hold over me anymore."

I told them the whole story. How I was Summer Slave to Ashlynn for her trendy clothes. The humiliating things I'd had to do.

"Why did you do all that?" Jazmine asked. "That sounds just demeaning."

"I wanted to start school with really cool new clothes," I said miserably. "And, honestly, I think I hoped some 'Ashlynn' would rub off too."

"Why would you want that girl to rub off on you?" Tess asked. "She was so mean to you and is going to be mean to us. And plus, she kicked a puppy!"

I might as well get it all out.

"Everyone thought she was such a star at camp," I said. "And look at her now. She *is* a star. She can sing, dance, and get boys to have crushes on her. You guys saw it yourself."

"She is pretty and talented—" Nick started to say.

"I know," I interrupted him. "You went to go look for her, remember? And then you went on a tour with her . . ."

Oops. That just came out.

"I wasn't going to look for Ashlynn," Nick said. "I was going to look for *you*. I told the chaperone I'd come with her to walk you back to the hotel."

Oh.

"And then she said she'd introduce me to the soundboard guy so I could learn some special effects," Nick said. "I wasn't going to hang out with her."

"Obviously, and it's on tape that he turned her down," Tess pointed out. "There's nothing to be jealous of."

"I'm not jealous," I protested. "Okay, I'm really jealous of her. And I thought wearing her clothes would bring me some of her . . ." What did Emma call it?

"Charisma!" Emma and Jazmine both shouted at the same time.

There. I'd said it all.

"So she has charisma," Tess said. "I wouldn't want Ashlynn as a friend. She's definitely no threat to you."

Awwww.

"I'm so embarrassed," I said, and sniffled. I couldn't even begin to look at Nick and see what he thought of all this.

"I'm so thrilled!" Emma said. "I've been trying to tell Payton this since the first Summer Slave chore. I think it may finally have sunk in, thanks to you guys. Payton, you were way too good for Ashlynn to humiliate you then and you're way too good to have her humiliate you now."

"It's true, Payton."

That was Nick!!! He smiled at me.

"Actually, I think I'm humiliated too," Nick said. "I think she only asked me out to get you jealous, Payton."

Wha . . . ?

"I told her I was there to pick you up," Nick said. "And I guess it was obvious that I, well, you know."

"Say it, Nick!" Emma cheered him on.

"I like you," Nick said.

!!!!!

Nick and I grinned at each other.

"Well, this has been a romantically disgusting TMI session," Jazmine said. "Can we get to the bottom line here?"

"You're right," I said. "The bottom line is I'm tired of feeling inferior to Ashlynn. I'm tired of her humiliating me, too."

"That's not the bottom line, Payton!" Jazmine rolled her eyes. "It's not all about *you*, Payton. Ashlynn is going to humiliate all the Geckos! And we need to Take. Her. Down."

Everyone cheered.

"Wait, wait," Ox said. "That's a little extreme."

"Ox is always the voice of reason." Emma nodded approvingly.

"She kicks puppies, and us," Hector said. "That's reason enough."

"Don't get me wrong, I'm an animal activist," Ox said.

"That's how he got his nickname 'Ox,'" Emma said. "His first campaign was in fourth grade, trying to save endangered oxen."

"*Awww . . . ,*" Tess and Hector and I said.

"Anyway." Ox cleared his throat. "Taking people down is not what the Geckos are all about. We play fair. But that doesn't mean we should do nothing. We can just go on the defense, not the offense. Let's think of it in football terms." Ox stood up and went over to the whiteboard. He picked up a dry-erase marker.

"In football there's defense and offense, right?" Ox said.

"No offense, but I don't have time to follow silly sports like football," Jazmine said.

"Sports are not silly," Emma said firmly. "Look at all of the leadership skills Ox is demonstrating right now! In fact, I think I should try a sport myself. I might excel in, perhaps, archery? Golf? Curling?"

"Maybe water polo," Tess offered. "I noticed you got in a few good shots at the pool."

"Just get on with this already," Jazmine huffed.

"It's an analogy, Jazmine. I would think if you can follow the binomial theorem, you can follow a football analogy," Ox said firmly.

"Yes, but how does this involve me?" Jazmine said. "And Hecky?"

"It's like a competition," Ox explained. "And whose side are you on, Jazmine? Team Ashlynn, on the offensive side, who made you play a wicked witch onstage?"

❀ 181 ❀

We all looked at her.

"Or Team Gecko, on defense, who is just protecting their teammates?" Ox said.

"Team Gecko," Jazmine said. Then she cleared her throat and spoke firmly. *"Team Gecko!"*

Emma and I looked at each other in wonder. I could see why Ox was team captain.

"Ashlynn went on the offense," Ox said. "She is trying to humilate all of us. But we're going to set up a defense. We'll block her every move. But we will do it, like my football coach says, with Good Gecko Class and Morals."

"Jazmine. Hector. Tess. Nick. Payton. And Emma," Ox said. "This is what we're going to do. . . ."

Twenty

HOTEL ROOM

I was in the bathroom of our hotel room doing my postcompetition ritual. (Which included brushing and flossing my teeth. For some reason there were always bowls of candy at competitions and I couldn't resist the gummy ones. Sticky.)

"Emma," Payton said, "are you finally finished getting ready for the theater?"

"Yes," I grumbled, opening the door.

"Oh," my twin said, looking at me.

"I know," I said, looking at her.

Looking at Payton was like looking in a mirror.

Because, for once, we were dressed identically. Our

hair was fixed exactly the same. We even wore the same shade of lip gloss. (Kiwi Smoothie Lipshine—I'd recommended it after noting in a magazine that it complemented fair-skinned blondes.)

"You look . . . um." I couldn't find the right words. Which was unlike me, as I had an extensive vocabulary.

"That bad, huh?" my twin said. She pulled me over to a mirror on the back of the door.

For a moment we just stared in silence.

We were both wearing the matchy dresses our mother had picked out. They were a hideous green.

"We look like twin green beans," I groaned.

"Yep," sighed my sister. "I wish I could wear my original theater outfit; it's so pretty. But there's no way I'm showing up wearing my Summer Slave dress."

"Anyway, remember, we're doing this for The Plan," I said, adjusting the itchy collar. "We have to look *exactly* alike."

"Well, we've accomplished that," Payton said. "Except I'm still one inch taller and my nose is bigger."

"And my hair is shinier," I teased. It was an old joke.

"Ooh! I just got a text from Tess!" Payton jumped.

"'P & E—where R U2? Come to lobby ASAP.'"

"What time were we supposed to meet everybody?" I asked Payton.

"I—um—thought Mrs. James said 4:four fifty-five," my sister said. "Or was it four forty-five? Oh, you know I'm not good with numbers."

"Identical on the outside," I said, grabbing the hotel room key, "but *not* on the inside."

"Yeah, well, we can't all be mathletes like you," my sister said as we raced for the elevators.

"So true," I said, pushing the down button three times. "I can't believe the mathletes competition is over already. I was in the math zone two hours ago, and then boom! It's over, gotta get to our next activity . . ."

"Yeah, the mathletes competition *was* pretty exciting," Payton said, leaning against the wall. "Even to me."

Ding! The elevator doors opened.

I got in and punched L for lobby.

"Pay! What are you doing?" I said. She was twisting around in a weird position.

"My dress is caught up on something," Payton said, tugging on it. She was still against the wall.

"Well, hurry!" The doors were closing. I tried to hit

the "doors open" button, but I didn't reach it in time. One minute I saw Payton, then the next I saw the inside of the elevator doors close shut.

Oops. Big oops.

Well, there *were* two elevators. She could catch the next one. On the ride down, I replayed some of the morning's competition in my head.

Ding! The doors opened on to the lobby. I got out and saw through a large window a bunch of my classmates standing outside. Ox! Tess! Nick!

Ding! I turned back. The second elevator had arrived at the lobby floor. I ran over to meet Payton.

"Emma!" Counselor Case and the trouble twins got out. "How are you doing?"

No time for small talk.

"Have you seen Payton?" I asked.

"Nope," Mason said.

"We'll wait down here while you find her," Counselor Case said.

"Thanks," I jumped into the elevator and pressed 8 for our floor. Just before the doors shut, Jason jumped in with me.

"What are you doing?" I asked him.

"I wanted to make sure you were okay," Jason said.

"I mean, about the competition results. I thought you'd be upset."

"That's really nice of you." I smiled down at Jason.

"I know *I'd* be really, *really* upset," Jason continued. *Ding!* Saved by the bell.

We got out on floor eight. No sign of Payton. "Quick, get back in," I said, pushing Jason into the same elevator. I hit L. The elevator started moving.

"Why are we going up?" Jason asked.

"Aack! We're not supposed to be," I told him. At floor ten, two businessmen got on. Then we started going back down again.

Ding! Floor 8. I leaned out of the elevator and yelled, "Payton!" just in case she was still on that floor.

"Emma!" I heard a small voice say. "Where are you?"

Our elevator doors closed. The two businessmen ignored Jason and me.

"I think Payton was yelling from the other elevator," I said. "Good, we'll meet at the lobby."

At the lobby, Counselor Case grabbed Jason's arm and said, "Stay."

"Where's Mason?" I asked, looking around.

"He went up with Payton when she decided to go

back up to get *you*." Counselor Case shook her head. "I couldn't stop either of them."

I turned to look out the large glass window that separated me from the rest of the Geckos. Why were Tess and Ox laughing? Like, hysterical laughing?

"Emma!" Payton said, jumping out of the elevator.

"Jason!" Mason said, doing a badly executed cartwheel into the lobby.

"Sheesh, finally," my sister said, and we quickly headed toward the exit, leaving the twins' mother to deal with them.

Yay! A revolving door! I got in and pushed. Payton got in on the next turn. And then Mason and Jason got in one together and *pushed*.

Yikes! The door sped up, and I stumbled trying to keep up with it. The boys kept pushing, so I missed my chance to exit. I was going around again. And so was Payton!

"Stop pushing, boys!" I screamed. "Let us get out!" I was practically jogging to keep up.

The boys stopped pushing.

Bam! I ran smack into the door that suddenly halted in front of me. *Ow!*

Bam! I heard what I guessed was Payton hitting the glass just like I did, only one compartment back.

I gently pushed enough to get out of the revolving doors of torture. My sister got out next.

"Whoa, I'm dizzy," I told her.

"Me too," Payton said.

"I don't think I'm injured," I said. "Just a little sore."

"Me too," said Payton again.

Together we wobbled over to Tess, Ox, and Nick, who were standing together.

"We're all here, Coach Babbitt!" Ox shouted into the crowd. Then he burst out laughing. Tess and Nick cracked up too.

"It's our dresses," Payton whispered to me.

"Hey, are you guys making fun of our outfits?" I came right out and asked. "Because they're the only identical things we had to wear."

Immediately the three of them stopped laughing.

"We're not laughing at your outfits," said Tess. "That's not it."

"No." Ox looked at me (Me!). "You look really pretty."

"You both look nice," Nick said a little shyly.

So the boys didn't recognize ugly dresses . . . that was kind of nice, actually.

"We're walking to the *theatah* now!" Mrs. Burkle announced. "Chaperones, is everyone accounted for?"

There were some grown-up yeses.

And we were off! Walking down the sidewalks of New York City. Payton and I formed a small group with Tess, Ox, and Nick. *Wait* . . .

"Tess, Ox, Nick," I said, frowning. "So what *were* you laughing about back there?"

"You twins," Ox said, "on the elevators. One comes out and goes back in with one smaller twin . . ."

"Then an identical one comes out of the other elevator, then goes back on with the *other* boy . . . ," Tess continued.

"And it's like one comes down, then goes up, and the other one comes down, and goes up . . . and you kept missing each other." Nick looked like he was trying not to laugh as he talked.

"And just when you thought it was done, you two get stuck in the revolving doors going around and around . . ." Tess snorted.

"Hey," Payton whined. "That last one hurt."

"Oh, sorry." Tess blushed.

"Are you okay?" Nick asked anxiously. (Ooh . . . he really *likes* her. . . .)

"I'm fine," my sister admitted.

"But we have both bruised our dignity," I concluded.

"Instant replay," Ox said to Nick. "Emma down, then back up plus one, Payton down, back up with twin two, both switching elevators, going left then right and left and right again."

"Then round and round . . ." Nick laughed.

"So how about our Gecko mathletes?" I shouted as loud as I could. *Complete change of topic necessary.*

"Cheers to our top individual scorer!" Ox yelled. "Miss Emma Mills!"

The crowd around us was now paying attention. They cheered loudly.

Suddenly Jason pushed his way next to me, dragging his mother, who was holding hands with his brother.

"It's not fair!" he wailed. "You were supposed to be the winner! Number one!"

"You know, Jason," I said, "that was tough competition we were up against. I am perfectly happy with being number three."

"And I'm happy, because number three is with me," Ox said, more quietly. And he held my hand! (Eeeeeh!)

"Well, I think number eight is pretty great." I smiled at Ox, who had come in eighth.

"Our school had four people in the top ten," Tess

said. "That's pretty amazing, with Nima number nine and Jazmine in fourth place."

Jazmine looked up when she heard her name.

"Whatever," she said. "The spelling bee and geography competition are coming up. I'll be winning competitions soon enough. Probably States and even Nationals."

I looked over at my twin. She looked at me.

I would bet that we were actually thinking the same thing. Twin moment! We *could* read each other's mind! Sometimes.

"I've been training for those for years," I whispered to Payton.

"I know. You're going to *rock* in the spelling and geo competitions," Payton whispered back.

"Exactly what I was thinking." I smiled at my sister.

Oh, boy. We were dressed identically and we had twin ESP going on. Things were getting a little too twinzy-cutesy.

"Let's not forget Hector at number eleven!" I said. Hector actually blushed. I was feeling generous.

"And the most exciting part of all," I continued. "We won the team trophy for highest overall scoring team!"

Nima held up her arm. It was her turn to babysit the trophy.

"Hurray!" I finished. "Woo-hoo!"

"Easy for you to be all happy." Jazmine shot me an annoyed look. "You beat us all."

"Hey," my sister said. "Emma's trying to celebrate your teamwork."

"Yeah, Jazmine," Nick said. "Either you're part of the Geckos team or you're not. We need to know before we carry out our plan. Are you in or out?"

Nick, Tess, Ox, Hector, Payton, and I looked at Jazmine.

"I'm on the team, okay?" Jazmine said. Then she yelled in a voice so loud it surprised us.

"Go, Geckos! We're number one! Go, team!"

Sydney came over with Cashmere.

"Is there cheering going on here?" she asked. " 'Cause it's nothing without an official Geckos cheerleader."

"Like Sydney!" Cashmere said, as if we didn't get it the first time.

"Great, Sydney!" Payton faked a smile. "You can lead us in a cheer."

"Yay!" Sydney clapped her hands. Then she added, "Not that I needed *your* permission."

"Go, Geckos!" she yelled, and did a cheerleader jumpy thing.

And everybody shouted, "Go, Geckos!" as we crossed the street in accordance with the pedestrian signage rules.

Suddenly, from out of the crowd, Mrs. Burkle's voice boomed loudly enough for half of Manhattan to hear.

"Look, everyone! Our twins are wearing identical gecko-colored dresses! Such school spirit!"

"More like gak-o colored," Payton said. "So embarrassing."

People were turning around to look at us.

"And we're still a block away from the theater," I muttered. "Operation Gecko Hick-o hasn't even begun, and already we have an audience."

"Shh!!!" My twin and Tess shushed me.

"We're here!" Mrs. Burkle sang out. "Get ready for a magical performance!"

"The performance of our lives," I said. This time no one hushed me. Or argued with me. Operation Gecko Hick-o was about to begin.

Lights.

Camera.

Action!

Payton

Twenty-one

AT THE THEATER

It was showtime!

The Dramatic Geckos and the Mathletic Geckos entered the theater together. Thanks to Mrs. Burkle's friend, we had part of the front row, second row, and third row blocked off for us.

I scanned the front of the theater to see if Operation Gecko Hick-o was in place.

Jazmine James was sitting in the very center of the front row, with her arms across the seats next to her. I grinned. Jazmine had some magic way of getting to the front-and-center seats in the classroom. She'd worked her magic here, too.

I texted our group:

Operation Gecko: Phase #1 Accomplished.

I went to sit in the third row, near the end of the aisle. Tess and Sam followed me in. We'd recruited Sam at the last minute, and he was totally happy to do his part.

The audience was all buzzing with excitement.

"I'm excited to see this play," Tess said as we sat down. Then she lowered her voice. "But nervous, too, about . . . you know."

I knew! I was nervous too, but feeling better as I watched the next stage of our mission happen. Ox took one of the seats Jazmine was saving. Hector sat down on the other side. Nick and Emma were nowhere in sight. And that actually was a good thing.

Everyone was in his or her place. I smiled that it had all gone so easily.

Until it didn't.

"Hey, there's Payton!" I heard a voice. "I want to sit with Payton!"

I saw Jason pointing at me. He was with his brother and his parents.

"Uh oh," I said quietly to Tess. "This could make things tricky."

I was nervous enough without my guidance counselor and the coach sitting right near me. And who knew what the twins would do nearby?

Jason ran up to me.

"Hi, Payton," he said. "I wanted to sit by you but Mason won't let me. He wants to sit in the front row because he thinks the star of the play is so pretty. He saw her picture in the program. Her name is Ashlynn."

That was the first time I was happy to hear about how pretty Ashlynn was.

"So I have to sit with them," Jason continued explaining. "Sorry!"

"I understand," I told Jason.

That was close. I sat back down in my seat. The rest of the audience was sitting down. And then the lights dimmed. The curtain rose. And *Fairytale Mash-up* started!

I forgot about everything else as I watched the actors and actresses onstage. The actors and actresses we'd seen onstage were amazing. And, I had to admit, Ashlynn was amazing too.

When Ashlynn sang her song about being a princess searching for her dream, I got chills.

"She's really good," I whispered to Tess.

Everyone was laughing and having a good time. And then they came to the part of the play that snapped me back to reality. The audience participation part. Nobody but Operation Gecko team members noticed Ox get up from his front row seat and disappear into the dark aisle. Or if they did, they probably assumed he was going to the restroom. But since Jazmine had snagged a seat so close to the stage, Ox was able to slip easily into his position behind the curtains.

"Audience participation improvisation!" announced the actor who had played a woodchopper in an earlier scene of the mashed-up fairy tales. He called up a boy I recognized from Emma's mathletes competition. Their skit was pretty funny. Then another actress called up a man who had to play her handsome prince. That was hysterical. The two guys sat down amid applause. It would have looked fun, except I knew what was coming.

And then it was Ashlynn's turn. She smiled sweetly. It was so weird how she could seem so sweet and nice onstage. And then in person . . .

"I'd like to bring up . . ." Ashlynn walked down into the audience. She turned toward me. I took a deep breath and prepared myself . . .

"You," Ashlynn said. She tapped Sydney on the shoulder with her princess wand.

"Me?" Sydney squealed. "Really?"

Really? Tess and I looked at each other.

"She didn't pick you," Sam said. "That's not in our plan!"

Well, okay. Our plan was foiled. But really, the plan was only in place because we thought Ashlynn was going to try to embarrass me. And the other Geckos. So maybe Ashlynn had taken a turn for the nice after all!

"But I wanted to take her down," Sam whined quietly.

"Our plan was defense," I whispered back. "So if she didn't go on the offense, we don't need to do anything."

Sydney practically skipped up to the stage. I started to think nicer thoughts about Ashlynn. Maybe she'd had a change of heart. Then Ashlynn suddenly stopped. And pointed her wand into the audience.

"Let's let one more person have some fun." She smiled. And she came over to me. And pointed her wand in my face.

There was no change of heart. It was still cold and black.

Tess's eyes widened. Sam grinned. Operation Gecko Hick-o was about to launch.

I stood up and pretended to be nervous. Okay, actually, I *was* nervous. Ashlynn smirked at me and I followed her up onstage.

"It's Payton!" Mason and Jason were practically

jumping out of their seats with joy as they waved at me. I smiled at them as I joined Sydney onstage. Sydney scowled at me, but I just pasted on a smile.

I could see Mrs. Burkle beaming at me from the audience. And then the house lights went dim, the stage lights went up, and I couldn't see anything past the stage.

"What's your name?" Ashlynn asked Sydney.

"Sydney Fish," Sydney said. "Future star!"

"What's your name, little girl?" Ashlynn asked me.

"I'm Payton," I said in my best clear voice. Mrs. Burkle would be proud.

"Sydney, in this improvisation scene you will play . . ." Ashlynn paused. "A tree!"

"A tree?" Sydney asked. "What kind of tree? A beautiful maple? A dramatic, tragic weeping willow? An apple tree that will feed the children?"

"A tree," Ashlynn responded.

"Well, what's my motivation?" Sydney asked her.

"Your motivation is that you stand there and be a tree," Ashlynn said.

The audience chuckled. They didn't know what I knew. This was going to be a humiliation attempt! I squinted to see if my Operation Gecko mates were in place, but the stage lights were too bright.

"And you," Ashlynn told me. "You are going to be a frog. A very *green* frog."

A frog! I was insulted for one split second. But then I realized how absolutely perfect that was going to be. I held back a grin so Ashlynn wouldn't suspect anything.

"Ew, a frog." Sydney laughed at me.

I pretended to be annoyed. I crouched down in a frog position. The audience chuckled.

"Hm, not just any frog." Ashlynn pretended to think. "How about an . . . insane frog?"

The audience laughed. I played a good sport. I tried to look crazy. I jumped around a little bit. And oops! Lost my balance and fell over.

"Heh." Sydney smirked at me.

Hey, it was a comedy and I was making the audience laugh. I knew Ashlynn was trying to embarrass me, but honestly, it was kind of fun!

"The story is, the frog—who, by the way, is covered with disgusting warts—thinks he is a prince and that a princess can turn him back into a prince," Ashlynn said. "So the frog will do anything the princess wants."

I could see where this was going.

"So I'm a Frog Servant?" I asked her loudly. And then I practically shouted. "I'm a *Frog Slave*?"

Ashlynn seemed surprised I was taking it so well. But I needed my voice to project realllly loudly.

"Why, yes." Ashlynn nodded. "My Frog Servant. Let's get into character *now*."

She waved her princess wand in the air.

"Frog Servant, I'm thirsty," Ashlynn said. "Fetch me a drink of water from my wishing well."

I crouched down and frog-hopped to the side of the stage. I passed Sydney, who was standing like a tree. I pretended to dip a cup in water and hopped back to Ashlynn.

Ashlynn drank it up.

"Oh, I forgot to tell you, Princess," I said. "I sipped it too. You might get warts."

The audience laughed. Ashlynn looked annoyed. But what could she do? It was a comedy!

"Hello, tree over here!" Sydney waved her branch—I mean, arm. "What about me?"

"Oh, your part isn't yet," Ashlynn said. "And shh, trees don't speak."

Ashlynn waved her arm and the lights over Sydney went off. She was in the back of the stage—in the dark! Obviously part of Ashlynn's revenge and humiliation.

"Frog, go bring me my glass slippers," Ashlynn commanded. I hopped one way, but Ashlynn stopped me. "No, that way!"

I hopped the other way, almost falling over. It was a challenge to hop like a frog. Ashlynn had me hopping all over the stage as she barked directions to me.

I started to huff and puff a bit. The audience cracked up at my frogginess. Ashlynn was starting to look pleased with herself.

"Frog, fetch me my wand," Ashlynn said. And she slid her wand to the side called "stage left."

And that's when we went into:

Operation Gecko: Phase #3

I hopped offstage to the left. I hopped past the wand, to behind the curtain, so the audience wouldn't see me.

And then, from the complete opposite end of the stage, like magic, I jumped out again.

Okay, it wasn't me! It was Emma! We were still in matching outfits, so it looked like I had magically gotten from one side of the stage to the other! I waited offstage.

Emma hopped over to Ashlynn and brought her the wand. Ashlynn looked confused but Emma smiled.

"How'd you do that?" Ashlynn sputtered.

The audience applauded.

Ashlynn then tossed the wand to the other end of the stage, stage right.

"Oopsie!" she said. "Fetch, Frog Slave!"

Emma quickly hopped across the stage without touching the wand, and kept going to stage right. I waited until she was hidden. Then, from stage left, I hopped back on. I grabbed the wand and brought it to Ashlynn.

Now she was really confused. How did I do that so fast?

The audience was cheering me on!

Emma went back to her hiding place on her side of the stage. I also knew Ox was there, standing in front of her to hide her. Hee.

Ashlynn's eyes narrowed. She didn't know what was going on, but she covered it up.

"Frog," she commanded. "There's one way to impress the princess enough to win her hand. And that is to sing for her."

"Sing?" I said, as if I were surprised.

"Yes, you must sing me a song," Ashlynn said. She turned to the audience.

"Every show of *Fairytale Mash-up*, we're going to have one lucky member of our audience sing!" she announced. "How cool is that? It's like our own *American Idol* showcase!"

The audience cheered. They thought that was cool. They didn't know I couldn't sing. But of course Ashlynn did.

I heard Sydney's voice pipe from the rear of the stage. "I'll sing! Yoohoo! I'll sing!"

But Ashlynn just had someone bring out a microphone and hand it to me.

I took a deep breath. I knew there were hundreds of people in the audience! All staring at me.

And I started to sing. And that was when:

Operation Gecko: Phase 4 went into play.

I couldn't see him, but Nick was backstage with the sound and lighting guy! The guy Ashlynn had introduced him to earlier that day. He'd asked if he could sit with him. And Nick asked him to turn off the microphone. And turn up the music way, way loud.

To drown out my horrible singing voice!

The music was so loud, the audience couldn't hear me singing!!!

I had planned to lip synch. But instead? I really sang. I sang on a this-close-to-Broadway stage in front of hundreds of people. And of course, they couldn't hear me. ☺

It was pretty awesome singing, knowing nobody could hear me.

Except that's when the howling started.

Aroooo! Arooooo!

I looked offstage, confused. Then I saw the Pomeranians! Bebe, Barbra and LeaMichele were here at the show too! Ashlynn's dog walker was holding the Pomeranians on a leash. And they were howling at me. Or maybe they were howling . . . with me.

Okay. My singing sounded like dog howling. I guess I should go back to lip synching.

"Frog Slave!" Ashlynn commanded. "Stop singing!"

The music cut off. And I spoke before Ashlynn could.

"Did I impress you?" I improvised. Then I sang in a horrible croak: "Ribbit!"

The audience cracked up again.

"No, that was terrible," Ashlynn said, really ticked off that I was getting laughs. "You don't win my hand. You have to stay a frog forever!!!"

"That's okay," I said. "I have my own true *frog* princess."

And from her side offstage, Emma hopped out. She hopped over to me and I gave her a hug.

"*It's twins!*" The audience roared with laughter! Then they broke out into huge applause! I could hear Mason and Jason yelling, "Go, Emma! Go, Payton!"

I saw the look on Ashlynn's face.

"You twins—" she hissed. "You—"

"Time to go!" I whispered to Emma. "Hop it!"

Emma crouched down low and I leapfrogged right over her. She leapfrogged over me until we were almost offstage. The spotlight followed us as we leaped away from an unhappy Ashlynn!

And the audience went wild clapping for us! It was awesome.

"Turn the spotlight back on me!" Ashlynn had lost her temper. The spotlight went back on her. And that's when it happened. Completely unplanned. Completely unscripted.

The spotlight shone on her shiny hair. And, boy, did she have shiny hair. I wasn't the only one who noticed.

Something leaped through the air and onto the stage. It leaped up higher and higher until it landed in Ashlynn's hair.

"Mascot!" Mason yelled from the audience. "My gecko!"

Mason's gecko had leaped into Ashlynn's hair. She was shrieking and dancing around.

The audience couldn't see the teeny gecko or hear him. But Ashlynn did. And she shrieked. And danced around some more.

And then the dogs spotted the gecko. And three

Pomeranians yanked free and raced over to Ashlynn. They were yipping and barking at the gecko! Ashlynn was dancing around, trying to figure out what was in her hair!

"Aack!" Sydney-the-tree shrieked. "What's going on? When is something going to happen to me?" The actor who played the woodchopper came back out onstage. Emma and I just watched from offstage. "Timber!" the actor yelled, and "chopped" Sydney down.

Sydney looked furious, as the audience laughed even more. Sydney fell down and sprawled on the stage. Like a dead tree.

"Wow, Operation Gecko Hick-o even brought Sydney down!" Emma whispered to me.

How appropriate. But now what? I had an idea!

I ran back on the stage and over to the microphone.

"So I, the magic frog, placed a crazy spell on the princess," I said into it. "I lived happily ever after with my Frog Princess, but this princess went insane."

That did it. The audience went wild.

"Curtain!" Ashlynn hissed. And the curtain went down but it didn't block the audience's applause.

Operation Gecko had its own real-life gecko! And a great group of student Geckos to make it a huge success!!!

Bravo!

Emma

Twenty-two

ON A NEW YORK STREET

We had one more surprise waiting for us.

"Please line up for the bus," Mrs. Burkle said.

"The bus ride home already?" we were all groaning. It had gone so fast.

"No." Coach Babbitt was grinning. "The bus tour around New York City!"

And not just any bus.

"Double-decker bus!" Payton and I both yelled. It was a two-story bus with an open top!

"Woooot!" I yelled louder, pumping my fist in the air—but Payton grabbed my arm and pulled it down.

"Too awkward?" I asked her. Payton nodded. Well,

209

maybe I'd never be a cheerleader, but I was a mathletes third-place winner! Woot!

"Twins on a double-decker bus." Mrs. Nicely smiled at us as she checked our names off her list as we boarded. "You can share some double memories on a double-decker."

"Remember the last time we took a double-decker bus together?" I asked Payton. "We were five and a half."

"That's so cute," Tess said from behind us in line. "I bet you guys were so cute when you were little twins."

"Yes!" Payton said. "We wore matching bright yellow dresses so Dad could spot us if we, well I, ran off. We sat together squished in a seat with Dad. And Emma corrected the tour guide on one of the facts—"

"I remember," I interrupted Payton, shaking my head. "The tour guide said that Andy Warhol was New York City's quintessential artist. But I said no way, it was Jacob Lawrence of the Harlem Renaissance. What was she thinking?"

"That you were annoying?" my twin said.

"More knowledgeable," I said firmly. Ha.

I followed Payton to the stairs. We definitely wanted to sit up top. So did everyone else, and there was a line going up.

"You don't want to sit with Nick?" I asked Payton. The two of them seemed to be getting along rather nicely, I had noticed.

"We should sit together," Payton said firmly. "Twins on a double-decker bus. Wait, is that okay with you, Tess, if I sit with Emma? Will you sit near us?"

"Of course! You're so lucky to have a twin sister," Tess said. "Someone who understands you. Someone who has shared all your memories since you were born!"

"Technically, since I'm six minutes and fourteen seconds older, I did have six minutes and fourteen seconds of my own memories," I pointed out.

"Emma, do you have to be so literal?" Payton sighed. "Besides, you don't have any memories that early on."

"Hello? I have a near-photographic memory," I said as the line moved forward. "I remember everything. I came out wondering and curious into the world. You were crying and needed a diaper."

"Okay, maybe I don't want to sit with you, after all," Payton grumbled.

"Oh, you twins," Tess said. "You're like a comedy team."

I started to take a seat in the front. I couldn't wait to hear the tour guide's fascinating facts.

"Oh, come on, the back is more fun," Payton said, poking me to move on. Then she grinned. "Oh, looky, Ox is sitting near the back."

Why, yes, yes he was. Sitting near the back. I stood up and followed her to the back.

"Emma," Ox said. "Sit here!"

Oh, yay. He pointed to the seat in front of him. Really pointed—with a giant foam finger with a baseball team on it.

"Got this from the street vendor," Ox said, poking me with the giant finger.

I had a sudden flashback of how I had been given the giant foam finger at our first Geckos pep rally. Everyone in the gym had looked at me and I'd had to lead a cheer in front of the whole school. Then I remembered that it happened during our twin switch. I'd been pretending to be Payton! Ox had thought he liked Payton, but it was really me. It was crazy! But look how it worked out.

Ox still liked me. *Me!*

"Give me that." I grinned and pulled the foam finger off his hand and put it on mine.

I stood up on the bus seat and waved the foam finger. *"Geck!"* I yelled out.

"What the heck?" Payton said, looking up at me.

"Geck!" I yelled out even louder.

"O!" Ox yelled back.

"Geck!" I waved the finger

"O!" everyone on the top floor of the bus screamed back at me.

"Nice spirit!" Ox said admiringly.

"Payton Mills, please do not stand on the seat!" Coach Babbitt called out. "Sit down and be safe!"

Oopsie!

"Hey, you just got *me* in trouble." Payton took the foam finger off my hand and bopped me on the head with it.

"Sorry," I told her. "But that twin mix-up is understandable. Of course Emma Mills wouldn't behave so crazylike."

"What have you done with my sister?" Payton asked me "You being silly in public?"

"Pht," I replied smugly. "That was nothing. I'm world-champion silly." And about to prove it.

Because that's when I saw Nima coming down the aisle toward us. She had been down in line at the street vendor when I had last seen her. And I'd given her some money for a few souvenirs.

"Here, Emma," Nima said, stopping in front of me.

She handed me what I'd asked for: two very tall foam hats as big as my head. One was a Statue of Liberty crown. I put it on Payton's head.

The other was shaped like the Empire State Building. I put that one on my own head.

"See? I can be frivolous in the spirit of good fun," I told her. "And fashionable, too! Thanks, Nima!"

I shook my head so the spiky top of the Empire State Building wiggled. We all laughed.

"Hey, there's Nick!" Tess waved for him to come back our way. Nick, Sam, and Reilly came down the aisle carrying giant bags.

"Whoa, Payton, Emma," Nick said. "Nice hats."

"It was a present from Emma," Payton said, and gave me a little hug.

"Well, Sam and I have a present for everyone too," Nick said, waving his bag in the air. "Street food!"

"Hot dogs! *Dosas!*" Sam started passing out food to people.

"Roasted nuts! Knishes!" Nick said. "Giant pretzels!"

Everyone was like, No way! This is awesome!

"Thank Mrs. James for the treats," Nick said. "She got them for us."

"Seriously?" We all craned our necks to see Mrs. James squeezing into the seat where Jazmine and Hector were sitting. Jazmine was reading the tour map. Hector was looking squished.

"Thank you, Mrs. James!" we all called out.

"Meh." She shrugged. "Jazmine thought we should feed the whole team. I don't know where that came from, but—"

"Thanks, Jazmine," I called up to her.

"Go, Geckos," she responded dryly, and looked back down at her tour map.

I took a pretzel. Payton took a *dosa* and Tess took a bag of honey nuts.

"Let's take a picture of us to send to Mom and Dad," Payton suggested. She pulled out my phone and held it up. "Say, NYC!"

"Mom and Dad will be thrilled to see us in our matching hats and dresses," I said, leaning in.

She clicked the picture just as Sydney and Cashmere came down the aisle toward us.

"Nice hats, twins." Sydney smirked.

"Nice hats, twins," Cashmere echoed.

I ignored them as they sat in the row ahead and across from us.

❀ 215 ❀

"Nice hats, twins!"

"Okay, enough!" Payton growled and stood up. But I grabbed her arm and dragged her back down. Because *Mrs. Burkle* had said that last one as she came down the aisle.

"Thank you, Mrs. Burkle," I replied, patting my Empire State Building spiky top. "Sydney and Cashmere had just complimented us on them too."

"I didn't know you had it in you, Emma," Mrs. Burkle said. "You're so free-spirited on this field trip. And perhaps you should join drama. Your frog was so convincing."

"Thank you," I said. "But I'll leave the drama to Payton."

"Ah, yes—Payton, improv at its finest!" Burkle smiled at Payton. "Perhaps a wee bit out of control, yes. But the audience loved you!"

Payton was beaming! She had even been asked for an autograph after the show.

"It has been a successful trip," I mused as Burkle went up and down the aisle doing a head count. "Not quite what I expected, but a successful trip."

"You didn't win the math competition, but you won the heart of Ox and an entire audience," Payton said quietly.

"Shh." I looked up, but Ox hadn't heard.

"You got to spend quality time with Ashlynn," I shot back. "And sing on a Broadway stage—so high-pitched it made dogs howl."

I smiled when I thought of the dogs. After the play Mrs. Burkle had told us that mathlete Ava had seen how poorly Ashlynn had treated the poofy Pomeranians. And Ashlynn's mother said enough is enough; the dogs must go! So Ava had texted her parents, who gave her permission to adopt the puppies!

"I can vouch for Ava's family," Coach Babbitt had told Mrs. Burkle. "They're very responsible and supportive."

"Then Ava will give the puppies the love they deserve," Mrs. Burkle had said. "Bebe, Barbra, and LeaMichele will want for nothing!"

I smiled.

"And, Emma," Payton said, continuing the teasing, "you got to be a frog and jump awkwardly around in front of hundreds of people. But seriously, you did get up onstage with no fear. Remember when you were petrified to in front of people?"

I did remember. I'd just about had a panic attack when I had to fill in for Payton, who was trapped under the stage looking for Mason's runaway gecko, in the school's *Wizard of Oz* play. But I'd actually been a decent Glinda the Good Witch. (Although what a relief when Payton emerged and took her rightful place *on*stage. She was a great Glinda.)

"You've really expanded your horizons at school this year," Tess said to me. "From fashion to being onstage to tutoring. What's up next for Emma? Spirit Club with your foam finger? Cheerleading?"

"Oh no, not Emma and cheerleading!" Sydney called out to us, groaning.

"Don't worry, Sydney," I called back. "I'm *not* cheerleading."

"You could play football." Ox leaned over to me and smiled. "With me."

"Actually, I'm still giving thought to water polo," I said. "Adding a sport will make me rather well-rounded."

"What about you, Payton?" Tess asked. "Are you going to try water polo with Emma?"

"Yeeps, no," she said. "I'm kind of thinking, though, of taking dance lessons. That way, if Drama Club does a musical, maybe I can be in it. Without tripping and hurting anyone."

"Speaking of dancing." Nick leaned over from his seat.

"Payton. Uh. There's homecoming coming up in a couple weeks. Do you, uh, want to go to the dance with me?"

"Yes!" Payton said.

Yay! Yay for Payton! I was about to say, but the bus horn went off.

Blarrrrt! Blaart!

"Please be *crackle crackle* seated," the tour guide's voice said over a loudspeaker. "*Crackle* We're off on our touronyorksty *crackle, pop*."

"They must be having technical difficulties," Nick said.

And then the bus took off down the street. I leaned back and felt the sun on my face. The wind blowing across my foam hat. Aahh . . . the sights and sounds of New York City.

"Mmmmmmble. *Crackle*. Mmmmble."

And the sound of a malfunctioning loudspeaker.

"I can't hear what the guide is saying," I complained. "All I hear is *mmble mmble*. How are we going to hear the fascinating facts about New York City?"

"I'm sure you already know every fact about New York City," Payton said.

"That is true!" I perked up. "I have a near-photographic memory for trivia.

"For example," I said loudly as we cruised through

Times Square. "Look over there. The LED electronic ticker tape displays letters and numbers that are ten feet high."

Payton groaned a little.

"And for you Dramatic Geckos," I said, forging on, "we're now passing the oldest Broadway theater, the Lyceum Theater, built in 1903."

I noticed people starting to quiet down and listen.

"And there's Bryant Park!" I pointed out.

"Oooh!" squealed Sydney from her row. "That's where Colin Christopher won season six of *Fashion Catwalk*!"

"I know!" Payton exclaimed. "I totally thought Lizzie had the best collection, though."

"Me too," Sydney agreed.

Then they both went silent. Sydney and Payton bonding? Awk. Ward.

"Ahem," I said. "Did you know that beneath the park is a storage area holding over seven million books?"

"Really?" Mrs. Nicely piped. "They should be out and available to the public! With all the literacy problems we face, we need to get books in the hands of as many people as possible!"

"Thank you, Mrs. Nicely," I said. "But look! We're at the New York Public Library, which holds more than seven million items that anyone is free to read!"

"Emma, remember when we visited that library? When we were five? I was scared of those two lion statues, but the librarian in the children's room was so nice I got over it."

"Oh yeah," I said. "Miss Robbins! She told us the lions were kind and brave, and their names were Patience and Fortitude."

"Spell those, Jazmine," I heard Mrs. James say.

"Mo-ther!" Jazmine whined. (She whined? Who knew?) "Oh-kay. P-A-T-I-E . . ."

"And here we are, already at Rockefeller Center," I continued. "Where the Top of the Rock offers a full three-hundred-and-sixty-degree view."

"Ugh!" Cashmere said. "Three hundred sixty degrees? That sounds really hot! And sweaty! Who'd want to go there?"

Silence from the mathletes.

"I'm guessing geometry is not Cashmere's strongest subject," Tess said quietly.

The double-decker bus was waiting for a light, to make a turn.

"Hey, did you know that goods that were worth twenty-four dollars—or a thousand dollars today—were traded to acquire Manhattan from the Native American Lenape tribe?" Ox said.

Yay! Ox facts rocks! I mean rock. I mean, his trivia facts are always interesting.

"What a bargain!" my twin sister said.

Sure. *Now* she enjoys trivia. When it's someone else's.

"After the Revolutionary War," Nima joined in, "the population exploded. From 1800 to 1900 it went from seventy-nine thousand to three million people! And now there are eight million New Yorkers in the city!"

"Of all cultures and personalities," Hector added. "Which is why I want to live here when I grow up."

"There's the Empire State Building!" yelled a lot of people. We all looked up. Whoa. Dizzying. I focused on more facts.

"Did you know that its high-speed elevators travel at up to one thousand feet per minute?" I announced. "And the world record for running up the 1,575 steps from the lobby to the eighty-sixth floor is nine minutes and thirty-three seconds!"

"Cool!" I heard people say. This was awesome! Finally my wealth of trivia was being appreciated!

"Emma." Ox leaned closer to me. "Do you want to go to the homecoming dance with me?"

I froze. Suddenly my tongue was tied.

"Er—em—yeh. That would be—lovely."

That would be lovely? Huh? Was I in a British historical novel?

"I mean, yes!" I regained my composure and smiled at Ox. (Ox!) Ox smiled back. (Ox's smile! So cute!)

"Well, okay, so there's Madison Square Garden!" I went back to my tour-guide persona. "And we know what *that* means!"

"Professional basketball!" Ox cheered.

"Pro hockey!" Sam and Reilly shouted.

"The Westminster Dog Show!" the eighth-grade mathlete Ava squealed.

"Yay! Yes! Woohoo!" yelled all the sports fans and dog fans. Which was basically everyone *not* in the James family. And me. I had actually been thinking about Penn Station, which was underground beneath Madison Square Garden and served six-hundred thousand rail passengers each day.

"Attention, Geckos!" Coach Babbitt turned around in his seat in the front and hollered back. "The bus driver apologizes for his sound system not working. He is willing to bring us back, and we can ride a different bus if you all wish to hear the tour facts from the beginning."

"No!" a whole chorus of kids yelled at once.

"Coach Babbitt, we like *this* bus tour!" Tess called.

"Keep this bus! Keep this bus!" people started chanting.

"I'll tell him everyone's happy," Coach called, and turned back around.

"Thanks to Emma and her cool tour-guide facts," Nick said loudly.

The people around me began a new chant. "Em-ma! Em-ma!"

I felt my face turn red. But it was a happy shade of red. Finally—*finally*—I was being appreciated for my passion for knowledge. And not in a competition, either. On a double-decker bus, in New York City, surrounded by my friends. And Payton's friends.

And Payton. Who was smiling at me. So I smiled back to make a mirror image.

Then I looked around and said, "You know what's made this tour—this whole trip—so great? It's all of you. All of us. Team Gecko!"

"Mmmble. Brooklyn *crackle* Bridge mmmble left," the loudspeaker said. We all looked left.

"Did you know—" I started to say.

"Did you know—" Ox said at the very same time.

We stopped and looked at each other.

"That the total length of the Brooklyn Bridge is 5,989 feet from end to end . . . ," I said, smiling.

"And it took sixteen years from conception to completion . . . ," Ox said, smiling back.

"And it was finished in 1883 . . ." I poked him in the side with the foam finger. He grabbed it off my hand and started poking me back.

"In 1883 . . . ," I repeated, squirming. It tickled so much, I couldn't finish my sentence.

"In 1883, the same year the Metropolitan Opera opened on Broadway," Cashmere said.

Cashmere? We all turned to stare at her.

"What?" Cashmere shrugged. "I like opera."

"Did I hear someone mention the Met?" Mrs. Burkle squealed. "I remember seeing the most exquisite performance of *Madame Butterfly* there. Of course, now the Met is located uptown in the same complex as the American Ballet Theatre and the New York City Opera!"

And then she burst into song!

"'Three little maids . . . ,'" she trilled.

"'From school are we!'" Cashmere sang, joining in with her.

"Who is this?" Mrs. Burkle shrieked. "What a beautiful soprano voice! Why aren't you in the dramatics club?"

"Um . . . ," Cashmere said. "Sydney says I have no star power?" Sydney sort of shrank down in her seat.

"Who is in charge of the dramatics club?" Mrs. Burkle yelled. "Me, Mrs. 'recognizes talent when she sees it' Burkle! You, young lady, will be our star in the next musical!"

Little gagging noises were coming from Sydney's direction.

"This is hilarious," my twin whispered to me.

"Could this tour get any better?" I whispered back. Then, *poke. Tickle.*

"Ox, quit poking me." I snatched the foam finger and bopped him over the head with it. But I was laughing, and so was he.

"You two," Payton sighed, "are perfect for each other. But you are starting to get on my nerves." She stole the foam finger out of my hands and rose out of her seat, almost standing.

She held the foam finger up high and yelled, "Go!"

But before anyone could yell "Geckos!" we heard a—
Thwap!

A big, leafy tree branch smacked my sister directly in the face.

Twenty-three

DOUBLE-DECKER BUS

Thwap!

"Gah!" I sat down in my seat, hard. "I'm okay. I'm okay. Phttt-ew!" I spit out a leaf.

"That thing just came from out of nowhere," Emma said consoling me.

"How, in the middle of New York City, do *I* get whapped by nature?" I complained.

I felt somebody picking leaves out of my hair.

"All gone, tree goddess," said Nick. "You sure you're okay?"

"Being called a goddess helps," I told him. "Yeh, it just stings a little."

"Then I have some good news and some bad news," Nick said. "The good news is you're okay. The bad news is—er—I happened to be filming everybody having a good time, and I—um—caught the whole tree-in-the-face thing on video."

"Aack!" I reached for his minicamera. "Delete! Delete!"

"No, keep it!" Sydney yelled. "Let me see it!"

"Hey, Payton," Emma said. "Lighten up. It's one more wacky moment from this trip."

Emma was telling *me* to lighten up?

"A *really* whack-y moment," my twin added.

"Okay, okay," I said. "Nick, you can keep it. As long as I didn't look *too* dumb. Did I?"

"You looked cute," Nick assured me.

That was nice, even if he wasn't telling the total truth. Although I hoped he was.

"You looked ridiculous!" Sam laughed.

"In the best possible way," Nick added.

"Look! Look! It's the Statue of Liberty!" somebody called from up front.

"We're at Battery Park," Emma said. "Just offshore is Ellis Island, where half of today's American population can trace their roots. Almost twelve million people passed through its gates as they immigrated here."

The bus slowed to a stop at the side of the road. We all posed for photos with the Statue of Liberty in the background.

When the bus began moving again, everybody with a camera phone started sending pictures.

"I'm sending one to Mom and Dad," I said.

"I'm sending mine to Quinn," Emma told me. "My friend Quinn. She couldn't come because she's not a mathlete or in drama."

"I *know* who Quinn is." I rolled my eyes. Emma was so proud of having her first real, non-competition-related friend. Actually, I was happy for her. "Tell Quinn I say hi."

We were all so busy sending and texting, we didn't notice when the bus began to head north.

"Looks like we're heading back," Emma said.

"This has been one pretty amazing trip," Tess said. "I'm glad I got to share it with you twins."

Awww.

"Oh, I don't want this trip to end," I said. "It's been so much fun."

Emma got a text on her phone.

"It's a text from . . . Mason?" Emma groaned. "Oh

no. He says he and Jason got their own cell phones from the giant Apple store. And now he can text me all the time."

Brrrrzt. Brrrrzt. Emma's cell phone kept getting texts.

"And apparently he means *all* the time," Emma sighed. "It's a picture text. What the heck is it?"

I peered over her shoulder closely.

"I think it's Mascot the gecko's eyeball," I said. "Extremely close-up."

"Ack!" Emma said. "Yeeks! Ick! Those boys are crazy!"

"You have to admit, they aren't boring." I laughed.

"That is true," my twin admitted.

The breeze blew through our hair, and the sun shone down.

"It's a good thing those twins aren't here," Emma said. "Because the ultimate sparkly, shiny thing is just up ahead. Mascot the gecko would have gone nuts."

"Wow, that skyscraper *is* beautiful!" I said.

"I have one more fact to share with you all before this tour is over," Emma said, speaking loudly in her tour-guide voice. "That is the Chrysler Building. It is considered one of the city's best-known buildings because of the shiny steel spire on top. But on the outside there are creatures made of steel as decoration. And you know what they are?"

Everyone was listening.

"Gargoyles!" Emma said.

"Like the home team at the mathletes competition?" Tess asked.

"Exactly." Emma nodded.

"Well, good-bye, gargoyles!" I called out as the bus passed the building. "And Go . . ."

"Geckos!" everybody shouted.

This time, no tree attacked me. So I said it again—"Go!"

"Geckos!" Everyone was cheering. Well, except for Jazmine James and her mother, who were looking at some sort of study-type book.

Well, some things never change. And some things I never *wanted* to change.

"You know, Emma," I said, "there may always be mean girls and confusing boys and middle school madness. But one thing I know is that I'll always have you."

"Awww," my sister said. "Payton, I don't say this often enough, but I am glad you are my twin."

"I love being twins too." I smiled.

"Even when you're called the wrong name?" Emma

asked. "Or when you get in trouble when I'm at fault? Even when you almost lost your chance at getting your first boyfriend because people thought he liked me? Or even when you're trapped under a stage while I perform— not very well—as your stand-in double?"

"Even with all that," I said, laughing. "And also when we have to answer stupid twin questions, and when people compare us to each other, and I have to say for the zillionth time that I have the bigger nose."

"What about hiding in the janitor's stinky closet?" Emma giggled, remembering where we'd first switched places.

"Okay, don't remind me." I shuddered. "Anyway, our switching days are done. In the past. No more trading places or faces. I'm Payton, and I like being me very much."

I had a flashback to the first days of middle school, when I tried so hard to be like Ashlynn and fit in with the popular girls. Wow. I had come a long way.

"Remember the first day of middle school, when I was so intense and socially clueless?" Emma asked. "And then we switched and both of our lives changed forever? You got drama and VOGS cast and Nick and Tess. I got to face my fears and get some balance in my life. And a real friend and a great boy-more-than-just friend. If we hadn't switched, I'd never have gotten to know Quinn and Ox."

"True." I nodded.

"So we probably won't have to switch ever again," Emma said.

"But if that's what it takes to help each other out, maybe—just maybe—we'd do it again?" I asked her.

"Never say never," Emma agreed.

"Just twins forever," I added.

And *that* deserved a twinky swear. We linked pinkies.

Who knew exactly what the future would bring? But as the double-decker bus pulled into Times Square, I was confident about one thing.

"Ready?" I asked Emma. She nodded.

"Twins forever," we both said. "Twinky swear." And we shook on it.

Acknowledgments

Thanks squared to:

The family: Greg Roy, Adam Roy, Dave DeVillers, Jack DeVillers, and Robin Rozines.

The Simon & Schuster crew: Bethany Buck, Fiona Simpson, Mara Anastas, Alyson Heller, Paul Crichton, Andrea Kempfer, Lucille Rettino, Bess Braswell, Venessa Williams, Karin Paprocki, Katherine Devendorf, and Angela Zurlo.

The agents: Alyssa Eisner Henken and Trident Media Group; Mel Berger, Graham and William Morris Endeavor Agency.

And: Mark McVeigh, Lauren Heller Whitney, Anna DeRoy, Anne Elisa Schaeffer, Daphne Chan, the Ginley girls, and Meridian and Adrienne.

And: Paige Pooler! Paige Pooler! Paige Pooler! (For three amazing book covers!)

Read on for more twin-tastic adventures
with Payton and Emma in . . .

Double Feature

By **Julia DeVillers**
and **Jennifer Roy**

Payton

One

ON THE MORNING SCHOOL BUS

Sunglasses! Did I remember to bring sunglasses?

I opened my tote bag and scrounged around looking for them. I felt my brush and mirror. My cotton-candy-flavored lip gloss. A chocolate-chip granola bar for after school.

And, phew, my sunglasses. I pulled out the pair of huge, round, white plastic sunglasses from my bag. I was going to need them after school for Drama Club. We were each supposed to bring a prop to fit the scene. My group was going to act out a scene on the beach, so I thought sunglasses would be perfect.

Plus they were cute. I slid my sunglasses on and

chilled, just looking out the window of the school bus. My sunglasses made it a little more challenging to see, but there really wasn't much to look at anyway. The usual houses, trees, people waiting for the bus. Definitely not as exciting as the bus I had been on earlier this week. That bus was a double-decker bus. In New York City!

Yes! I went to New York City with the Drama Club. We went to see our drama teacher's friend who was producing an almost-on-Broadway show. It was amazing! We went on the double-decker bus and toured the city. We also went to a giant toy store, stayed in a cool hotel room, and swam in the hotel pool.

And if that wasn't amazing enough . . .

We got to go onstage in the off-Broadway show! It was almost like we were Broadway stars!!!

Oh, and by we, I mean me and my sister, Emma. My twin sister. Emma and I look pretty much exactly alike.

I'm PAYTON, the twin who:
- is one inch taller.
- has slightly greener eyes.
- is dressed quite fashionably in her black T-shirt with the word "Broadway" across it in glitter, skinny jeans, and tall

boots and is sitting in the back of the bus, where it's coolest to sit because it's bumpy. (And farthest away from the bus driver, of course.)

Emma has the opposite opinion about where to sit on the bus. Emma always sits in the front seat for everything—buses, classes, and even the front seat of the car. She always wants to be up front and first for everything.

I'm the twin who likes to chill in the back. Unless there's a stage involved. Then I want to be front and center. Yes, I love acting. I love being in Drama Club at school and in school plays. And when my parents let me do two clubs, I could be on camera for VOGS club. VOGS is the school's video news show.

My parents made me stop doing VOGS, though, because I bombed a test and a quiz in English. Sigh. My parents told me I had to choose between Drama Club and VOGS until I could get my grades back up. I chose drama, but I also want to be in VOGS. I loved being on the school news show and had turned out to be kind of good at being on TV. My English teacher, Mrs. Burkle, was also my drama teacher, so I was hoping to extra-impress her at Drama Club today. It couldn't hurt!

I pictured it now.

"Payton, your acting is so fabulous that I will also give you extra credit in English class!" Mrs. Burkle would say. "A++!"

Okay, unlikely, I know. But at least I still got to be in Drama Club.

Emma wasn't in the Drama Club or VOGS. But somehow she kept getting sucked into performing onstage and on-screen—usually pretending to be me. It had happened our very first week of school. It had happened in our school play. And it had happened on our trip to New York City.

This last twin switch was pretty epic, not only because we were on an almost-Broadway stage. We also got to get back at this girl Ashlynn who was trying to humiliate us and our classmates on our school trip.

I had been surprised to see Ashlynn. She lived in NYC, so I hadn't seen her since she tortured me at summer camp last year. Ashlynn had pretty much turned me into her slave, making me clean things in exchange for her hand-me-down clothes. At the time I'd thought it was worth it so I could look cool in middle school. Let's just say it didn't work out as planned.

But we prevailed in New York City, and now

Ashlynn would never bother me again—*muah-ha-ha!*

"Why are you making those weird cackling sounds?" A girl who had just boarded the bus stopped in the aisle and looked at me. Oh. It was Sydney. She wasn't as bad as Ashlynn, but let's just say she's not my biggest fan.

During the first week of middle school I'd thought Sydney would be the cool kind of friend to have. She was already the center of attention, had great clothes, and seemed to know all the cutest guys. Instead, she'd turned out to be a major mean girl. Especially to me. She turned on me after an incident where I'd tripped at lunch and my burrito went flying and oozed all over people.

Anyway, Sydney usually didn't ride my bus. I hoped she hadn't moved to my neighborhood and would be riding my bus permanently.

"Move," she commanded two kids who were sitting in a back seat across the aisle from me. Because she was Sydney, they obeyed and scrambled out to sit somewhere else. Sydney slid into the seat and stretched her legs out, putting her feet (in cute olive espadrilles) across the seat so nobody would sit there.

"Well, hi, Payton," Sydney said. Hmm. Sydney and I had become temporary allies versus Ashlynn in New York City. So maybe things had changed for the better.

I cautiously said hi back.

"Those kids thought they were cool enough for the back seats. *Pfft*, I don't think so," Sydney scoffed. "But apparently, Payton, you think you are. And you think you're so cool that you even wear sunglasses on the bus."

Things had *not* changed for the better. I reached up to take my sunglasses off but realized that she'd know I cared what she said. And I didn't. *La la la, ignore.* I kept my sunglasses on. I did, however, tell myself not to make that cackling sound again. I dropped my hands and pretended to be busy looking for something important in my bag. Yes, very important.

"Are you wearing sunglasses because you think you're a major star now?" Sydney kept going. "A glamorous off-Broadway star?"

La la la, not bothering me at all.

"Or," Sydney kept going, "are you wearing sunglasses so people won't recognize you? After you and your twin totally embarrassed yourselves on school TV when you got in that huge fight, I don't blame you for trying to hide."

Oh, ugh. That was weeks ago! I was hoping everyone had forgotten about that disaster. Emma and I had started our middle school careers as the twins who had switched places, fooled everyone until they were busted, and been filmed on school television making complete idiots of themselves.

But that was supposed to be totally in the past. And I wanted to keep it that way. So I changed the subject. And if there was one topic of conversation that could distract Sydney, it was . . . Sydney.

"Sydney, why are you on my bus?" I asked her.

Sydney's face lit up.

"I slept over at my aunt and uncle's house," she said. "For a seriously exciting reason. A seriously exciting *secret* reason."

I didn't say anything.

"But if you want to know"—Sydney leaned over—"I'll give you a clue."

"That's okay," I said. "I don't need to know."

I shrugged and went back to fake-searching my tote bag. I'd gotten much better at learning how to handle Sydney. If there was something Sydney hated, it was being ignored. I leaned back in my seat so she would know that I really didn't want to know about her excitingly secret secrets. (Although I was curious.) (But *so* not worth it.)

"Payton?" Sydney gave me her squinty look. "Payton?"

Ignoring you, Sydney. Doo dee doo.

"Payton? Why is your twin sister waving her arms around freakishly?" Sydney was no longer looking at me, but toward the front of the bus.

Sydney knew just how to get me to un-ignore her.

I leaned forward and looked up the aisle. Sure enough, I could see the top of my sister's head and her hands waving wildly around above the seat. Oh no, what was she doing? I thought about ignoring her but I noticed people were also leaning forward to look at her. I pulled out my cell phone and texted.

E! Chill. Hands down.

No response. I could still see Emma's hands waving around in the air for some unknown reason. Sigh. She didn't realize it, I was sure, but she was embarrassing herself. And not just herself—us. Here was one of the major problems with being an identical twin: People didn't always know who was who. That meant people could be thinking that it was me in the front seat. Me, Payton, waving my hands wildly around and making a scene.

She must be stopped.

I fastened up my tote bag and left it on the seat so nobody would try to snag *my* back seat. I couldn't let Sydney rule my bus entirely. I did my best to ignore her as I slid out and walked up the aisle.

There went Emma's hands, waving. I could hear people cracking up as I walked up the aisle. I picked up my pace to stop her as soon as possible. However, I'd forgotten I was still wearing sunglasses, which meant I couldn't see very well. For example, I didn't see somebody's violin case sticking slightly out into the aisle until I tripped over it. I stumbled forward just as the bus lurched into a left turn.

Ack! I grabbed on to the closest seat back and accidentally yanked somebody's ponytail.

"Ouch!" The ponytail owner yelped. Loudly. Unfortunately, that meant pretty much everybody on the bus looked away from Emma's hands and saw me trip and stumble my way up the aisle, out of control. And anybody who hadn't looked yet definitely did when the bus driver yelled at me.

"You! In the sunglasses! Sit down while the bus is moving!"

I felt my face turn bright red. I quickly sat down on the edge of an empty seat and waited until the bus became more stable. Then I ducked down and half-crawled up the aisle toward my sister, trying to stay under the bus driver's radar.

I slid into the seat next to Emma, which was open because the only other person I knew who liked to sit in the front seat for everything was Jazmine James. And her mother drove her to school every day.

"Why hello, Payton," Emma said calmly, her hands now in her lap like a normal person's. "What are you doing up here in the front of the bus?"

"I'm here to ask you to stop waving your hands wildly," I whispered. "The whole bus can see you and it's embarrassing."

"More or less embarrassing than stumbling up the aisle, yanking somebody's hair, and getting yelled at by Morris, the bus driver?" Emma peered at me. "While wearing oversize sunglasses on a bleak day?"

Agh! I slumped back on the seat in defeat.

"I was hoping you didn't notice my approach," I said.

"Of course I saw it. I see everything on this bus," Emma said. She pointed to a large mirror that was attached to the back of the bus driver's seat. "I convinced Morris to angle an additional mirror so that I can monitor the goings-on of my fellow bus mates. This way I can alert him to any shenanigans."

"Are you serious?" I asked her.

"Oh, she's very serious," the bus driver chimed in.

"Oh, Morris, does this mean I can speak now?" Emma called up to the driver.

"No," Morris replied.

Emma saluted him and made a "zip up her lips" motion.

What the heck?

"I'm no longer allowed to speak to Morris when the bus is moving," Emma explained. "I had been trying to help him out by telling him about shortcuts he could take. I also alerted him when he was waiting too long for a student, which might put him behind schedule. And I told him when people behind us were causing distractions."

"She was very distracting," Morris grumbled.

Emma sighed. "So we made a deal that I could stay in the front seat if I didn't talk to him without him calling on me first. I came up with the idea to wave to him to alert him when I have valuable information to share."

The bus turned into a neighborhood as Emma continued speaking.

"So I'm honing my nonverbal skills in the process. Did you know that spoken language is less than one-third of our communication? Most of our feelings and intentions are sent through body language." Emma waved her arms wildly, I guess to demonstrate. "Or hand gestures." She gave me a thumbs-up. "And facial expressions. For example, I'm copying your facial expression right now, Payton. It's a cross between a scowl and a look of frustration. Thus, I'm inferring that you are irritated by something."

"Or someone." I sighed. Morris the bus driver sighed too.

Morris probably ignored Emma half the time, like Dad did when Emma sat in the front seat and tried to tell him more effective driving methods. Emma likes to point out when things could be done better. Yes, it could be annoying. But I had to admit, she was almost always right.

The bus slowed down and pulled up to a bus stop. A bunch of kids got on the bus.

"Okay, I get it," I told Emma. "But can you not wave your hands so very wildly? It looks pretty spazzy and we can even see you all the way in the back. People might think you're me."

I hoped she would get the hint that she was embarrassing us.

"And, Payton," Emma said, "would you mind following the bus safety rules by not walking while the bus is in motion? People might think *you* are *me* breaking a rule. That would be so embarrassing."

I groaned. I couldn't win.

"And speaking of spazzy," Emma continued, "people are still talking about you stumbling down the aisle."

"How do you know that?" I asked her.

"I can see them in the rearview mirror." Emma pointed. "As you know, I've been practicing reading lips. That girl with the slate-gray stylishly tied scarf just said something about how you're wearing sunglasses on the bus like you're a TV star. And then she laughed, remembering how we got into that fight the first week on school TV."

I groaned again. This was not going as planned.

"I'm going back to my seat," I said.

"If you need to tell me anything else," Emma said, "just wave your hands wildly from your seat and get my attention. Then mouth it. I need more practice reading lips."

"Can't you just use twin telepathy?" I tried one last-ditch effort. "Practice reading my mind instead?"

"Payton, shh. You're not supposed to be talking to me out loud, remember?" Emma replied. Then she mouthed something at me that I completely didn't understand.

I felt defeated as I slid my sunglasses off and waited for the bus to stop so I could go back to my seat. The bus slowed down and pulled to a stop and the doors whooshed open. I stood up and started walking to the back. But not before I saw Emma's hand go up and wave.

"Yes, Emma?" I heard Morris say.

"You don't have to wait for him," Emma replied. "He's a minute late and you're already two minutes behind schedule."

I looked out the window to see a boy in my Drama Club, Sam, running madly to catch the bus. I turned back to Emma.

"Sam is carrying a prop for our Drama Club skit," I said to Emma. "It's slowing him down. Give him a break."

Sam was carrying a beach chair that was big and awkward. I was glad I had only brought sunglasses. I waited at the front to make sure Emma couldn't convince the driver to leave him.

"Made it!" Sam said, huffing and puffing as he climbed up the steps.

"An extra one minute and twelve seconds delay," Emma said, shaking her head.

I sighed as I stood up and followed Sam down the aisle. It was slow going, as he banged into people with the beach chair as he passed by.

"Can I go ahead of you?" I asked him. "I already got yelled at by the driver once for being in the aisle."

"Sure!" Sam said cheerfully, and as he stood to the side he knocked another person on the side of the head.

"Sorry," I told them. "Sorry!"

I was relieved to slide into my back seat without stumbling or pulling anyone's hair myself.

"Are you okay?" Sydney asked. "I saw you falling all over the place."

Ugh. I had forgotten all about Sydney being on my bus. I slid my sunglasses back on so I could ignore her.

"Did you bruise anything?" she continued in a voice of mock concern. "Or just your ego?"

A few seconds later I had a brief moment of happy karma when Sam made his way to the back and tried to sit with Sydney. When she told him the seat was saved, he got up and the beach chair accidentally knocked her on the side of the head.

"Can I sit with you?" Sam asked me.

"Sure," I said, and moved my tote bag. Sam tried to

wedge himself and the beach chair into the seat. It was a tight fit.

"Sorry to squish you," Sam apologized.

"It's okay," I said. "Well, if you could get the top of the chair out of my stomach it will be okay."

"Sorry." Sam shifted the chair. "This bus is lame. It would be cool if we could have a huge double-decker bus like we went on in New York City."

"I know! That bus was cool," I said. Emma and I had sat on the top out in the open air.

Brzzzt. Bzzzt.

Speaking of Emma, my cell went off. Emma was texting me.

Look up and say something. I angled the mirror 76 degrees so I can read your lips perfectly.

I shook my head, my lips tightly closed.

Brzzzt. Bzzzt.

Shaking head doesn't count! Say something! I want to prove to u my mad lip-reading skillz.

I mouthed: *You are bizarre.*

Brzzzt. Bzzzt.

You said "You are star!" ☺ *Twin-kle twin-kle little star 2 u!*

Sigh. I started to slide my phone back into my bag.

Brzzzt. Bzzzt.

What now? I pulled up her text and read it.

But you may want to take off your sunglasses. They're kind of embarrassing.

Ag. I gave up.

Emma

Two

ON THE WAY TO SIXTH-PERIOD STUDY HALL

My lip balm! Did I remember to bring my lip balm?

I slipped my hand into the outside pockets of my backpack. I felt my mechanical pencils (eraser side up), sticky notes (sticky side up, ew), and my extra scrunchie. A cinnamon-raisin granola bar for after school.

And, whew, my lip balm. I pulled out the vanilla-flavored stick from pocket #4. Normally, I didn't wear any cosmetics. Unless Payton forced me to wear lip gloss on "special occasions." Which, for her, was every day at school. Or at home. My twin sister was a lip gloss expert.

I, however, was a lip-*reading* expert. Well, not exactly an expert—but I was picking it up pretty quickly. Like on the bus earlier this morning, I could tell that people were talking about my twin's massive wipeout on the bus. Not by listening, but by reading their lips!

Although you couldn't miss their laughter.

Anyway, Payton may be a little spazzy, but she's my best friend. A few weeks ago I might have said she's my *only* friend in my peer group. But then middle school happened. Now I had friends. And I was back in my familiar environs. Yup. It was going to be a normal day.

"What's the capital of Loserland?" a familiar and unwelcome voice said behind me. "Millsville!"

I turned around.

Jazmine James!

"Get it? 'Cause your last name is Mills?" A boy's voice.

And her sidekick, Hector!

"And that's where Emma will be after the geography bee." Jazmine cackled. "Millsville, Loserland!"

Sigh. I turned around from my locker. Besides making friends in middle school, I'd also made a few enemies. I leaned back casually. *Don't let her get to you.*

"Still hurting after I annihilated you at the mathletes competition?" I faced Jazmine and Hector. "The competition that I *won*?"

"Oh, please." Jazmine waved dismissively. "That was so last weekend."

Last weekend we were in New York City! Now we were back to the usual routine. Which I liked. "Predictable" was my favorite word. Besides "winner."

Riinnnng! The warning bell rang.

"Well, lovely talking to you, but I must go," I said, shutting my locker door and turning to head to study hall . . . *YANK!*

"OW!" I shrieked as I was slammed backward into my locker. My ponytail. I'd closed my locker on my hair. I tugged. Nothing happened. I was stuck. I was stuck in my locker.

"Heh," said Hector. Then he and Jazmine burst into hysterical laughter and went off down the hallway. Jazmine's long braids swung freely down her back and she treated the hall as her personal catwalk, elbowing people out of her way when they got too close.

Grrr. Jazmine James. From Eviltown.

"Hi, whichever twin you are!" a girl called to me as she walked by.

"Uh—hi!" I said. I leaned back against my locker, so maybe I'd look like I was hanging out. *La la la, keeep moving, folks. Nothing to see here.*

"Hi, Payton!" another girl said to me.

"Er—hi!" I said. Thanks to a public humiliation after our first twin switch, Payton and I had become rather well-known. Although most people couldn't tell us apart. But hey, that was good in this case. They could think my *twin* was plastered to her locker. Payton, not Emma.

"Hey, Emma!" my friend Quinn greeted me.

"Quinn!" I yelled. "Can you, um, come here for a second?"

Quinn stopped and frowned a little.

"Can we talk later?" she asked. "I don't want to be late for class."

"Please?" I begged.

Quinn came over quickly.

"I'm stuck," I admitted. "My hair is stuck in my locker."

"Ow, does it hurt?" Quinn asked, looking concerned.

Note to self: Friends don't laugh when you're in trouble. Unlike Jazmenemies.

"Only if I move," I said. "I tried to pull it out, but I got nowhere."

"Okay," Quinn said. "What's your locker combination?"

"Great idea!" I told her the numbers. And I tried to smile, in case the people walking by saw me in this stupid situation. The very last thing I wanted was for people to think "stupid" and "Emma Mills" at the same time.

"Forty-nine . . . sixteen . . . three," Quinn repeated. I heard the wheel spinning. "How do you remember your combination? I'm terrible remembering numbers."

"The square root of forty-nine is seven minus the square root of sixteen, which is four, equals three," I said. "Did it work?"

"Oh, sorry, I forgot to turn it twice," she answered. "What was it again?"

I told her. Perhaps even merely a month ago, I would have rolled my eyes. But having a nice friend like Quinn had upped my social skills from "zero" to . . .well, improving.

"Got it!" Quinn said triumphantly, and I heard a *click*.

"I'm free!" I said, shaking out my ponytail. Crisis over.

"Yay," said Quinn. "Now I've gotta go. Can you hang out after school?"

"No." I sighed. "I'm tutoring today." I thought about my new outlook on friends. I wanted them. So I made sure Quinn knew I wasn't just blowing her off.

"Quinn, I want to hang out, so let's plan something

more fun than rescuing me from a—er—hairy situation. Like a Boggle tournament or the mall."

Quinn smiled and nodded as she left.

Well, I handled that well. Considering I'd been stuck in a locker, that is. Which, yikes, made me late for study hall! I rushed to study hall. Fortunately, it was in the same hallway as my locker. And since I had to tutor Mason and Jason, the Trouble Twins, after school, I needed every spare moment to study in study hall. I was on an intense study mission for my next competition: the Geobee! The schoolwide competition was Friday night and I was going to be ready for it. *Geobee, geobee, geography is fun for me . . . especially when I win.*

And with that happy thought, I walked into study hall just in time before the last bell rang. I had exactly forty-three minutes to prepare for the competition. I planned to answer every question correctly. Emma = 100 percent winner!

Real life. Real you.

design your own lip smacker

talk to girls around the world

play games and send e-cards

take fun quizzes and polls

create a customized profile

ask miss smackers a question

enter a sweepstakes

find new lip smacker flavors

read and write book reviews

share your creativity

check out movies and videos

Jammed full of surprises!

LiP SMACKER®
LOUNGE

VISIT US AT WWW.LIPSMACKERLOUNGE.COM!

DOUBLE TROUBLE
JUST TOOK ON a WHOLE
new meaning....

Do you love the color pink?
All things sparkly? Mani/pedis?

These books are for you!

From Aladdin
Published by Simon & Schuster